Tori was no dummy.

He just might be crazy enough to shoot. She tossed the bedroll at his feet and threw her hands up with as much attitude as she could muster. Arching her brow, she spat out, "So what? Is there an ordinance against sleeping outside?"

"Give me awhile, and I'm sure I can find one." Billy Ray glanced down at the bundle, then back up at her. That's when he noticed what she was wearing. "You're wearing your nightclothes!" he charged with something akin to horror.

"Well, that's what a lady does when she's about to go to bed! Miss Rachel said so!"

"Nelson, you don't know nothing about being a lady if you think tromping around in the great outdoors in your nightclothes is proper!"

"Why you—you. . ." She stumbled on her outburst as she tried to think of a word to call him that wasn't on the list of words Rachel had told her she couldn't use. Coming up sadly empty, she said the first thing that popped into her mind. "You mean man!"

Her pause must have been too lengthy, for he was already bending down, shuffling one hand through the blankets. Of course he was diligent to keep the gun firmly trained on her.

"Find anything interesting?"

He stood, scowling. "There's nothing in there."

"I never said there was."

They stared at one another for a second, and Tori could tell his mind was whirling with confusion. "Can I put my hands down now? They're beginning to hurt."

His lips thinned in a grim line. "Not just yet!" She sighed and tried not to think about them. "If you weren't stealing something, you must have been trying to escape," he surmised.

Clearly he isn't the brightest man in the world. "In my nightgown?" she asked sarcastically, hoping her expression said what she was thinking.

KIMBERLEY COMEAUX has been married twelve years to Brian who is a music minister, a songwriter, and formerly the lead singer for The Imperials. They have an eight-year-old son named Tyler. The family of Americans currently resides in Ontario, Canada. Kim turned her attention toward writing Christian fiction when she discovered songwriting wasn't for her, because she loves to read, especially romance. "I started out with an idea, and before I knew it, I'd written a book-length story."

HEARTSONG PRESENTS

The Sheriff
and the Outlaw

Kimberley Comeaux

Heartsong Presents

A note from the author:
I love to hear from my readers! You may correspond with me by writing: **Kimberley Comeaux**
                                      Author Relations
                                      PO Box 719
                                      Uhrichsville, OH 44683

ISBN 1-58660-488-0

THE SHERIFF AND THE OUTLAW

Cover illustration by Lorraine Bush.

PRINTED IN THE U.S.A.

one

Springton, Texas, 1893

The silver star on Billy Ray Aaron's leather vest flashed in the early summer sunlight as he strode confidently through the downtown street. His hand reached up to touch it for what must have been the fourth or fifth time since he'd pinned it on that morning, just to assure himself that it was there and it was real. As of today, Billy Ray was Springton's new sheriff, and it was his first official day on the job. He'd always known he'd be a sheriff. He just never dreamed it would be in this town—his hometown—the town his great-grandfather had started years ago.

The sheriff before him, Leander Cutler, who had held the position for eight years, had married a local girl and was raising two fine twin boys. Billy Ray had just assumed Lee would remain as sheriff for years to come.

So after serving as Lee's part-time, then full-time deputy, and after convincing his brother, Bobby Joe, he did not want to help run the Aaron-family sawmills, he'd decided to look for a sheriff position in another town. Just a month ago, on his twenty-fifth birthday, Billy Ray was just about to accept a job outside Fort Worth, when Leander surprised him by announcing that his father was ill and he and his family were moving down to Houston to help his brother run the family ranch.

The town council had unanimously voted for Billy Ray to take his place.

So, today, it was with mixed emotions he attended his friend's going-away party. He was there officially to keep the peace but mostly to let Lee know how much he appreciated all that he'd taught him and done for him.

"Howdy, Sheriff. How's your first day on the job, so far?" the former sheriff drawled to his friend and successor, breaking Billy from his musings.

He smiled and shook hands with Lee, then reached out to give Lee's wife, Patience, a quick hug. "It's been about as eventful as sittin' in on the ladies' quilting circle," Billy Ray quipped as he patted their twin boys' blond heads. He glanced around at the large crowd. Folks from near and far had gathered to say their good-byes to the former sheriff. Lee Cutler would be missed; there was no doubt about it.

"Well, that's Springton for you," Lee commented. "We've had a few exciting moments, but all in all, this is a pretty calm town. Nothing much happens here."

Billy Ray grinned teasingly, glancing from Lee to Patience. "I don't know. I think the most exciting moment was when you both got locked up in the jail!" he said, referring to the time a prisoner escaped, locking them both up in one of the jail cells. It had been the event that made Lee realize he was in love with Patience. They married a short time later.

Patience quickly hid her embarrassed smile. "Shame on you, Billy Ray! I don't think we need to bring up that again!"

"Just let him talk, Patience," Lee said, his eyes narrowing. "One day a young woman is going to come along and shake his life up like you did mine. And when it happens, I'm going to be on the first train up here to see it!"

Billy Ray just grunted. "When I get married, it's going to be someone who's a lot like this town—nice and calm."

"Sheriff!" A desperate female voice arose from the crowd. "I've been robbed! Help!"

Instincts made both the former and present sheriff jump into action. Patience, however, grabbed her husband by the arm, stopping him.

"Hold on there, Sweetheart. We've got a train to catch. Let Billy Ray see about it. He's the sheriff now," Lee's wife gently reminded him, causing the former lawman to grin sheepishly.

"You're right." Turning to Billy Ray, he patted him on his shoulder. "Well, so much for calm. Looks like you're on your own, Buddy."

Billy Ray smiled at his friend. "Have a good trip, y'all, and God bless." Quickly, he embraced them both before running in the direction of the still-screaming lady.

Betsy Duron, who was dressed from head to toe in more pink ruffles than Billy had ever seen, was in quite a state by the time he reached her side. "My purse is gone, Billy Ray—I mean, Sheriff. One minute it was on my arm, the next minute it wasn't, and I can't find it anywhere!" she wailed, falling limply into his arms.

Billy Ray, having been raised in an all-male household most of his life, was at a loss as to how to deal with the weepy woman. Awkwardly, he patted her on the back with one hand, while pulling out a freshly laundered hanky with the other.

"Now, don't go on like that, Miss Duron. Are you sure

you just didn't drop it somewhere?" He managed to push the hanky into her hands and back away from her a few steps.

"Yes," she replied between hiccups. "I looked but didn't see a thing."

He pushed his hat back on his head as he glanced about them. "I'm sure it'll turn up. Someone probably found it and picked it up. Why don't we—"

"Sheriff!" Another voice cried out, only this time the voice was distinctly male. Billy Ray looked up to find Harold Norton jogging his way.

"What's the matter, Mr. Norton?"

"Someone done went and stole my pocket watch!" the elderly man told him as he tried to catch his breath. "Had it attached to my belt buckle and tucked into my overalls pocket, but now it's gone!"

The folks around them overheard what they were saying, prompting them to check their own valuables. "My brooch is missing!" someone yelled.

Another called out, "I can't find my wallet!"

Pretty soon, several people were making similar claims. There were too many to dismiss as absentmindedness or clumsiness!

Unbelievably, there was a pickpocket in their midst.

Quickly, Billy Ray started scanning the area, asking his brothers and a few others who had gathered around him to help look for any new faces in the crowd—someone who might appear suspicious.

Finally, one lady reported she'd seen a boy of about her average height dressed in ragged, dirty clothes and wearing a brown cap pulled low over his face.

Billy Ray tried to keep everybody quiet about what they were doing so that they wouldn't scare the boy away, but in a town where everybody knew your business and gossip spread like wildfire, it was impossible. Soon, everyone was scurrying about, some even yelling for the boy to come out and give himself up!

"What a mess," Billy Ray murmured to himself, unaware that his eldest brother and his sister-in-law were standing right by him.

Bobby Joe chuckled. "You're right about that, little brother. Whoever it was is probably well hidden by now."

Susannah reached out to take hold of Billy Ray's arm. "Now, don't you go and worry about a little bitty old setback like this. You're a good lawman. You'll catch him before the day's out!" she announced loyally in her Southern drawl.

"Don't baby him, Susannah. He could've stayed with me at the sawmill and not had to worry about this at all. But he's made his career choice, so just let him be," Bobby Joe scolded with a mock gruffness. At one time, Billy's choice to be a lawman instead of helping his family with the sawmill was a sore subject with him and his oldest brother. Now, Bobby Joe, having finally come to accept Billy's choice, could joke about it.

Billy Ray snorted derisively. "One little pickpocket ain't going to cause me to worry. Susannah's right. I'll catch him before sundown."

Bobby laughed and opened his mouth to speak but closed it again when something caught his attention just over Billy's shoulder. "You might just do it before that, little brother. I just saw someone peek out of one of those barrels by the saloon, and he was wearing a cap."

Billy turned to look where Bobby Joe was pointing and saw the barrel begin to tilt to one side. "I'd better go see to it before the kid falls out and hurts himself."

"Watch yourself, Billy Ray. You don't know if he has a gun or not," Susannah called out fretfully as Billy Ray began to walk swiftly toward the saloon.

Billy waved to her that he was fine but kept his attention focused forward. His instincts were on keen alert like they always were when he was involved in catching a criminal. He withdrew his pistol and slowed down, easing toward the barrel.

"Alright, I know you're in there, so why don't you slowly stand up. No one will hurt you if you'll just do as I say," he ordered in a coaxing yet firm voice, his gun trained steadily on the wooden container.

Not a peep sounded from the barrel, so Billy gave the warning again. Still nothing.

He got ready to cock his gun, reached out his hand, and slowly began to reach for the lid.

All of a sudden the barrel tipped forward, knocking Billy Ray to the ground. The boy scrambled out and over the sheriff, stomping hard on his stomach.

Stunned with pain, Billy Ray tried to grab the boy's foot but found he could barely move. Seconds seemed like hours as he tried to regain the breath that had been knocked out of him. Bobby Joe ran up to help him, motioning for the other two Aaron brothers, Daniel and Tommy, to chase the thief.

Bobby managed to finally get Billy on his feet, but he was still clutching his aching belly. "You alright?" Bobby Joe asked his little brother. "He didn't break any ribs, did he?"

Billy gritted his teeth and managed to stand up straighter, putting on a braver face than he felt. "I'm fine, and it wasn't my ribs he stepped on, it was my gut!"

Bobby laughed, slapping his brother on the back. Billy's teeth gritted harder. "Let's go and see if Daniel and Tommy have rounded up the pickpocket yet," Bobby directed, leaving Billy to follow him.

Unfortunately, Tommy and Daniel had managed to lose the boy and had no idea where he might be. They formed a small search party and looked around for most of the afternoon, but the young thief seemed to have disappeared.

Finally, Billy sent them all home, telling them to keep their eyes open and let him know if they spotted the boy.

Before he went home, Billy stopped in at his office and sank down onto his heavy wooden desk chair. He leaned back, stretching out his long, lanky body, then ran his weary hand through his thick brown hair. The movement caused a pain to rip through his gut. Wincing, he sat up straighter and tried not to think about how much worse it was going to hurt in the morning.

For a moment, Billy Ray looked around the office and on the other side of the room at the jail cells. It was all under his command now—a big responsibility, yet such a privilege and honor. It was a position he'd prayed for, and God had heard his prayer.

Now, his prayers would be centered on guidance and direction. He wanted to be able to be fair and just, but he also wanted the folks in Springton to know there was someone looking out for them and protecting their families and businesses.

Yes, it was a big responsibility. But with God's help, he was more than ready to take up the challenge.

He was in the process of looking through some new wanted posters when the door flew open and Harold Norton came stumbling into the room, out of breath as usual.

"Sheriff, come quick. I just saw the thief go into the mercantile! I'm afraid he might hurt my wife," Harold told him, his voice worried and rough.

The chair bumped against the wall as Billy hurriedly stood up and started toward the door. "Go to the mill and get my brothers, Harold. Tell them I might need them for backup." He quickly studied the elderly man, who appeared as though he was going to pass out. "And please take my horse. You're going to give yourself a stroke running around like that!"

He left the office and walked across the street to the mercantile, pulling his gun from his holster, as he tried to see the boy through the store window.

He spotted him at the back of the store, so he carefully opened the mercantile door, wincing when the hinges creaked; then the bell above the door began to jingle. Billy might as well have yelled out that he was coming in, because all that noise had the same effect. The boy peeked over a shelf. The sheriff was startled to see a pair of shockingly blue eyes, set within a very dirty face, peering at him.

It was a strange moment, but it was quickly forgotten when the boy shot toward the back of the store. Billy was quick to follow but was stopped short when Adelaide Hayes Norton, the shopkeeper, said to him, "I locked the back door, Billy Ray; he ain't going nowhere!" A look of excitement had her cheeks flushed and her eyes flashing. Miss Addie always did like adventure!

He nodded his thanks to her and slowly went through the doorway that led to the back storeroom. He caught the thief trying to open the door. His movements were frantic, and Billy Ray could have sworn he heard the boy whimper.

He's scared, Billy realized, feeling kind of sorry for the cornered pickpocket. "Now, hold on there, Fella," he said in a coaxing voice. "There's no way out, so you might as well stop fighting it." He walked a little closer as the boy froze, still facing the other way. "I've got a gun, but I won't have to use it if you'll just turn around and let me take you back to my off—"

"No!" the boy screamed in a high-pitched voice as he whirled around and charged at Billy like a wild animal.

This time, Billy was ready—or at least he thought he was. He managed to grab the boy, twirl him around, and yank one arm behind his back. When the thief started to try to wiggle free, Billy wrapped his other arm, his gun still in his hand, around the boy's shoulders. He was trying to figure out how to exchange his gun for a pair of handcuffs without losing his grip on the boy when the thief bent his head down and bit Billy's arm.

Surprised, Billy's grip loosened, making him drop his gun. Billy quickly got a better hold on him this time, forcing the outlaw to the floor, face first. When the boy tried to grab the gun, the sheriff beat him to it and knocked the weapon out of harm's way.

The whole time they'd scuffled, the boy hadn't said a word, so Billy was surprised when he cried out. "You can't do this," he whimpered, his voice high-pitched and shaky.

"My brothers will hang you out to dry when they hear about this! I can't go to jail; I just can't. . ." His outlaw choked on the last word as if he were sniffling back tears.

Billy was taken aback not only by the pleas and the tears, but also by the voice. He sounded more like a girl than a boy!

He couldn't be, Billy reasoned. *Could he?* He finished cuffing him, then gently pulled the slight, stiff body up into a sitting position. Downcast eyes refused to look at him when he crouched down to have a closer look.

Billy Ray took in the small features, the long eyelashes, and the plump curved lips hidden behind all the dirt. His eyes traveled down the dusty coat and pants that were hanging too loose on the slight frame.

He swallowed hard as he reached out to the cap, determined to find out what was underneath. The thief jerked away to stop him, but Billy already had ahold of it and pulled.

It wasn't the long blond hair, which tumbled free, that finally convinced him of the truth. Oh no, it was the all-too-female glare that was directed at him—the same glare he'd seen his sister-in-law give his brother on occasion—that gave him the final proof.

His outlaw, the thief and pickpocket who had thrown the whole town into an uproar today, was a *woman!*

two

"Who is that?" Daniel, Billy Ray's brother, asked as he, Tommy, and Bobby came into the room along with Addie and Harold Norton.

"Why our pickpocket's a girl!" Miss Addie exclaimed in amazement.

"She's the one we've been looking for all day?" Tommy blurted out, aghast.

"I ain't no thief!" the girl all but growled at them. "Let me go. You ain't got no proof of nothing!"

She tried to stand up, but Billy grabbed her by the shoulder and pushed her back down. With his other hand, he dove into her bulging coat pocket and pulled out a handful of jewelry, coins, and other trinkets. "I'd say we have plenty of proof!" he returned.

She tried to wrestle from his hold, but with her hands shackled behind her back, it didn't work. "Those are mine. Leave them alone!" she screeched.

Billy just shook his head and stood, pulling the girl up with him. "Let's go. Maybe after you spend a night in jail, you'll reconsider your story."

"Now, hold on there, Billy Ray!" Addie admonished as she stepped forward with her hands out. "You're not going to lock this poor child up, are you?"

Billy Ray fought to control his patience. At the rate his stomach was throbbing, and now his arm from the bite the girl had given him, he was running low on politeness. "This 'child' stole from half the guests at Lee Cutler's going-away party today, Miss Addie. She's an outlaw and will have to see the judge tomorrow. But until then, she goes to jail!"

He started to move forward, when all three of his brothers stepped in front of him. "Do you think you need to handcuff her like that?" Tommy spoke first.

"Yeah, look at her, Billy Ray. She's crying." Daniel bent toward her and gave her the smile he gave most females when he wanted to be charming. Outlaw or no, she was still a woman and apparently not immune to his brother's tactics. "What's your name, Darlin'? Where's your family?"

After giving Billy another hateful glare, she sniffed a little, then turned to his brother and actually smiled. "My name's Tori Nelson, and I ain't got no family. Not around these parts, anyway."

Her soft answer caused everyone, except Billy, to look at her with compassion and pity.

"Why you poor little girl," Miss Addie crooned as she came up and patted her shoulder. She looked at Billy sternly. "Now, Billy, I know you've got to do your job, but why don't you just let her stay with me and Harold tonight? We'll bring her by the courthouse in the morning."

Tori looked at Billy with so much hope and expectancy, he nearly gave in. There was something about the girl—maybe it was her eyes that stirred something in him.

He shook his head and looked away. Then again, maybe he was just so tired he wasn't thinking straight.

"I'm sorry, Miss Addie, but the law's the law." He started to pull Tori past his brothers and into the main part of the store when the bell over the door jingled and in walked Reverend Caleb Stone and his wife, Rachel.

Billy groaned inwardly when he saw Rachel look at the girl. At this rate, he was never going to make it to the jail.

"Sheriff! What's going on? Why is this poor girl in handcuffs?" Rachel started in right away, just as Billy Ray knew she would.

Billy held up a hand. "Now, don't you start fawning all over her, too, Miz Stone. She's the pickpocket we've been looking for today. She's going to jail, and that's that!"

"Why don't you let me take her in and I—"

"Miz Stone, I—" he tried to interrupt when the girl suddenly interrupted him!

"Oh, please don't let him take me to jail. Please help me! Please!" she wailed as a whole new crop of tears welled up and started making more dirty streaks down her face.

Billy closed his eyes and took a deep breath. She wasn't going to get to him. She wasn't! "Whatever y'all have to say, you can take it up with the judge tomorrow. Until then, she goes to jail!"

Pulling her along, he brushed past the preacher and his wife and walked out of the store, determined no one was going to stop him.

He just didn't understand it. How could anybody have pity on someone who'd made a rug of his belly and a pork chop of his arm? No sane person, that was for sure. But he hated to admit to himself, he did feel sorry for her. And he wondered. . .pondering where she came from and how she came to be the thief she was. Wasn't there a family who cared for her? Wasn't there a friend who could have taken her in?

But those questions wouldn't be answered tonight. She

was crying too much, and he knew by the looks she'd sent his way, she wouldn't be inclined to tell him anything anyway.

He was the enemy.

As he escorted her across the street to the jail, it seemed to Billy the whole town had come out to gawk. A few threw out comments about him arresting a woman, but he ignored them all. Sometimes the job of a lawman wasn't pleasant, but it had to be done. Lee had taught him that.

But it still didn't help him feel better when he took the handcuffs off her and closed the door to the cell. And when she looked at him, he saw the most haunted and lost look he'd ever seen in someone's eyes. It gave him the most insane urge to put his arms around her and tell her everything was going to be all right.

Instead he turned, walked back to his desk, and sat down—feeling almost guilty, as if it were *he* who had done something wrong instead of this outlaw named Tori.

❧

Victoria "Tori" Nelson slumped down onto a cot that was set in the corner of the tiny cell and buried her head into a small, fluffy pillow. For thirteen years she'd been living on the streets with her brothers, learning survival methods only the very desperate and the very lost learn. She'd come close to being caught before but had always managed to elude capture—until today.

She never should have gone into the store, and she wouldn't have, except that she'd seen the pretty doll displayed in the window. Suddenly a flood of memories crowded her mind of a time when she'd had a doll just like the one in the store. A time when her mother and father had been alive. A time when she'd been happy and cared for. A time that ended when she was only six.

Tori had gone into the store to just have a look, when she'd spotted the sheriff through the window. She ran to the back of the store to hide, but when she peeked over the top of the shelf, she saw he'd come inside looking for her. Trapped!

Now her future depended on a judge and the sentence he would serve her. She had no idea what the penalty for stealing was in this county, but she hoped against hope that he would find some sort of mercy for her in his heart.

She sat up then and looked at the man who'd done this to her. He didn't look like most lawmen she'd come across. His brown wavy hair looked clean and combed, for one thing, and his face wasn't full of whiskers. There was no chewing tobacco packed in his cheeks, nor was there a spittoon nearby.

And there was something strange about his blue eyes. Maybe it was the way he'd first looked at her. She'd felt funny inside, like something was happening that would affect the rest of her life.

She snorted with disgust. Something happened all right. She was sittin' in a cramped jail cell in some hole-in-the-wall East Texas town, when she should be headed on to the next town.

The sheriff glanced her way, catching her glaring at him. He shook his head and looked away as though she were something beneath his attentions. He was like most lawmen in the respect that he was so judgmental and self-righteous. The man didn't seem to care that he had just ruined her life. He could have let her stay in that nice woman's house, but instead he locked her up as if she were an animal that no one wanted.

She would never forgive him for this, and she promised herself she would never, ever forget.

❧

If someone had told the sheriff what would happen the next day when the girl's case was brought before the judge, he would have never believed them.

Maybe it was Rachel Stone and Addie Norton's fault. They'd come calling early the next morning with a wash-tub, a dress, and all kinds of female contraptions and potions Billy couldn't identify. He'd been ordered out of his own office—and the door firmly bolted behind him—for at least an hour.

Who knew that once the girl was all cleaned up and out-fitted in a pretty green dress, she'd turn out to be as pretty as she was. Her face was slightly tanned, and there was a pink tint to her cheeks that made her light blond hair and incredible blue eyes stand out all the more. Her nose and mouth were delicate and small, much like those of the porcelain dolls his niece played with. She was slim in build and of average height, but still there was something fragile about her.

Which was ludicrous, really. Especially after the tussle she'd given him both times he'd tried to arrest her.

But for some reason, everyone who had been a victim of her thievery forgot how upset they'd been and the trouble they'd gone through to help look for her.

When she began to pour out the story of her life—how a train wreck had killed her parents, how her two older brothers had taken charge of her and, with no money, tried to raise her—it was hard not to be touched by her words. Eventually, her brothers had turned to stealing what they needed and had taught Tori to do the same. Two years ago, her brothers were arrested and sent to a prison in West Texas. Tori had managed on her own for all that time, doing the things they'd taught her to do—picking pockets and stealing.

It was all she knew. The only way she could survive.

By the time she'd finished her sad tale, there wasn't a dry eye in the room. Even his tough-as-nails brother Bobby Joe looked like he would like to break down and cry. So, it was no surprise when not one of her victims was willing to press charges against her.

Billy, who'd watched the whole drama from the back of the courtroom with great skepticism, finally stepped forward.

"Judge Denton, can I say something?"

The judge, who seemed at a loss as to what to do next, nodded his head and motioned for Billy to speak.

"There may not be anyone here who is willing to press charges, but it doesn't change the fact that several crimes were committed. I found the stolen goods right on her person. We can't just let a known thief walk out of here!"

A buzz of whispers sounded about the room, some in agreement and some not. As the judge banged his gavel on the bench to order silence, Billy Ray glanced at Tori and found her staring at him with the same hurt, haunted look in her eyes he'd seen the night before. He tried to look away, but something about the girl drew Billy, disturbed him in some way.

"You're right, Sheriff. But I'm not sure that putting this

young woman in jail would be the right thing to do in this situation," the judge returned, breaking Billy from his thoughts and giving him the initiative to look away.

Billy Ray shook his head in confusion. "Then what would you suggest, Your Honor?"

"I have a suggestion." Rachel Stone spoke as she walked toward the judge's bench. "From my conversation with Miss Nelson, Your Honor, I learned that she has never been taught what is right and what is wrong. Ever since she was six, there's been no female influence and no moral figures in her life. No one has even shared with her about God." Rachel looked over to her husband, who gave her an encouraging nod. "I want to suggest that Tori come and live with us. We can teach her about morals, manners, and how to act like and become a respectable young lady. She can learn a good work ethic by helping us with the orphanage, also. Most of all, Your Honor, we can share the love of Christ with her. And I think we all know how accepting Christ into one's heart can change a person completely."

The judged nodded his head, apparently contemplating what Rachel had said. He turned to Tori, whose attention had been fixed on Rachel and what she was saying about her. It was as if she couldn't quite understand what the preacher's wife was trying to offer her.

"What do you have to say about this, young lady?" the judge asked Tori. "Some folks don't like others helping them out or someone trying to change them, whether it's for the better or not. I'll make it your choice. For three months you can stay with the Stones, obey their rules, cooperate with them, and learn whatever they set out to teach you—or you can spend three months in the county jail up in Tyler."

Tori looked from the judge to Rachel. The two women stared at one another for a few moments, and an understanding seemed to pass between them because both of them smiled. "I want to go with the preacher and Miz Rachel," Tori said, her voice full of relief and a little hope.

Billy couldn't believe what was happening! "Now, hold on here, Your Honor! What kind of sentence is that? She'll cut out of here the first time the reverend and his wife turn their backs!"

Once again those blue, condemning eyes blazed in his direction, but this time he wouldn't look directly at her. The law was the law.

"Do you have a better suggestion, Sheriff?" Judge Denton asked as he peered over his spectacles, his bushy gray eyebrows raised in question.

"I say the three months in jail just might teach her a lesson!" he stated righteously.

"Shame on you, Billy Ray!" his sister-in-law, Susannah, admonished from her seat near the front of the courtroom. The outspoken redhead stood and came forward, placed her hands on her hips, and stood toe to toe with Billy. "Everybody deserves a chance in life! You were practically born with a silver spoon in your mouth, so you have no idea what it must be like for someone to grow up without a home!"

"And you do?" he flung back at her. Her background was more privileged than his was!

"No, but Rachel knows what it's like to be given a second chance, and if anyone can help that girl, it's her!" she retorted, glaring at him with the look she always gave her disobedient students when they got out of line.

"Well, so be it!" the judge called as he banged the gavel once more. "Victoria Nelson, you are to be handed over to the custody of the Reverend and Mrs. Stone for a period of three months. If you do not abide by the rules they will set for you, or if you try to leave town during this time, you will be arrested and taken to the county jail, where you'll serve the rest of your term. Is that clear?"

A look of pure joy and amazement filled Tori's face as she looked at the judge. "Y–yes, Your Honor," she stammered.

Irritated the judge had sided with the girl, Billy shook his head with disgust and started out of the courtroom.

"Now, hold on there, Sheriff Aaron! I'm not quite through," the judge ordered, his voice booming. Billy let out a long breath and turned back to the bench. "During this time, it will be up to you to check up on this young woman to make sure she's doing what she's supposed to. And during the last month, it will be your turn to teach her about the law—what to do and what not to do. For one month, she'll come to you daily for thirty minutes at a time. It'll be up to you to choose what you want to teach her."

Horrified, Billy sputtered, "But—but, Your Honor, I—"

"Are you trying to tell me you don't want to do your civic duty by teaching this unfortunate girl how to be a law-abiding citizen?"

Well, since the judge put it that way, what could he say? Billy glared at the girl who had turned his first day as sheriff into a nightmare he'd not soon forget, then looked back to Judge Denton and nodded. "I'll do it, Your Honor."

"Court's adjourned!" The gavel sounded with finality as it hit the hard wood of the bench.

I'll do it, Billy Ray thought to himself, meeting the girl's happy gaze head-on with his disgruntled one, *but I certainly am not going to like it!*

three

Since most of Tori's nineteen years were spent in the company of her brothers, she didn't quite know what to make of Rachel Stone and Susannah Aaron. Rachel kept smiling at her and telling her she was going to be "just fine" as they walked to the house behind the church, and Susannah chattered nonstop in such a thick Southern accent that Tori couldn't really understand what she was saying.

But Tori wasn't concentrating on what either woman was saying. Her eyes kept straying to the scowling sheriff who was walking alongside them with a rifle propped on one of his broad shoulders.

The man was just like those mean mongrels that had arrested her brothers—small-town lawmen who were just itching to fill their jail cells and make themselves look like heroes. She'd even heard it whispered that this was the sheriff's second day on the job. It figured!

It didn't matter that he was sort of handsome or that he carried himself like some sort of Texas prince. And so what if he had the bluest eyes she'd ever come across! They sure weren't very pretty when they were glaring at her as if she were a pesky rodent in his way!

Her eyes lit on his muscular arms and broad shoulders. If only he'd been a skinny man she might have gotten away. As it was, she was a little proud she'd given him as much trouble as she had.

In fact, since the judge had pronounced her sentence, the sheriff hadn't looked anything but mad! Though Tori wasn't sure how she'd accomplished it, she felt that she had somehow won a major victory and he'd been the loser.

It was a good feeling.

"Billy Ray, I declare!" Susannah suddenly exclaimed. "Are you going to follow us all the way to Rachel's house?"

Billy nodded grimly as he hoisted the rifle to the other shoulder. "All the way and then some. I aim to keep a sharp eye on their place the whole three months."

Tori narrowed her eyes at him as he glared back at her. "You could put a hun'erd guards around the house, and I'd still be able to escape if I wanted. I ain't scared of you none, Lawman."

Susannah's eyes widened with dismay. "Goodness, gracious! We're going to have to work on your grammar, honey child, the very first thing we do!"

"That will be your department, Susannah. I'll work on her hair and wardrobe. Why, have you ever seen such pretty hair? I think—"

Rachel's comments were interrupted when Billy stepped in front of them. "Do y'all honestly think that by teaching her how to talk and how to dress you're going to really help her?" he snapped, waving a hand in Tori's direction.

Tori had had enough of his insults. She may not be very polished or sophisticated, but she was still a person. True, most of her life had been spent on the wrong side of the law, but that was the only way she and her brothers knew how to survive. Tori yearned to be different, however. She wanted to be a lady like Susannah and Rachel. She craved having folks look at her with respect. She dreamed of living a normal life in one town with a man who loved her.

Those had been only unrealistic wishes—until now. Now she could see some of those things happening to her, and she wasn't about to stand by and let this mean man say she couldn't accomplish it!

"You just wait, you mealymouthed varmint! I'm gonna be a proper lady if I hafta work day and night ta do it!" She walked closer to him, with her hands on her hips, just as she had seen Susannah do earlier, until they were practically nose to nose. "This is my chance to make somethin' of myself, and I ain't gonna let you or nobody else ruin this for me!"

They glared at one another for a full five seconds with all the irritation and ire that had been building up since they met. But then. . .something changed. She suddenly became aware of how close she was standing to him. . .of how his breath was blowing on her lips. And for the first time she saw him not as the sheriff but as a man. A very handsome, strong man.

His eyes seemed to darken for a moment, and she wondered if he was feeling the same strange emotion she was experiencing.

But the moment was quickly gone when his eyes widened with shock. He recoiled as if she were a skunk about to spray him. Pointing his gun at her, he sputtered, "You just stand back, Woman!"

Outraged, she railed, "I didn't do anything, you idiot!"

"Honestly, Billy Ray! Put that gun down before you hurt somebody," Susannah ordered sternly as she came and put her arm around Tori.

"You do seem a bit flustered, Sheriff. Why don't you go

on back to your office and take a rest," Rachel told him in her smooth, yet emphatic tone.

Billy Ray looked a little sheepish as he lowered his rifle. "I guess I do have a few things to do. But I'll be checking back with you tonight," he added quickly, all the while avoiding Tori's eyes.

"We thought you probably would," Rachel answered with a grin. "Good-bye."

The two women led Tori around Billy Ray and toward Rachel's house. Tori tried not to look, but she found herself glancing back over her shoulder to where the sheriff was standing. To her surprise, she found him staring right at her.

Quickly, she jerked her head back around, embarrassed he'd caught her looking back.

But then again, I caught him staring at me too!

Now, *that* was a really good feeling.

That good feeling, however, vanished the minute she began receiving instruction from Susannah and Rachel.

"I have to take another bath?" Tori asked, aghast, as Jessie, Rachel's teenage son, poured water into the huge tub that occupied the center of a bedroom.

"Honestly, Child. You would think taking a bath was something you only do once a month!" Susannah teased as she shooed Jessie out of the room and stepped over to Tori to start undoing her dress.

"Every two months was too much for me!" she mumbled as the dress flew over her head. "Can't you get sick or something from too much bathing?"

Rachel smiled her serene smile. "That's an old tale straight out of the Middle Ages. Where did you hear such a thing?"

Tori tried not to be embarrassed as they undressed her and practically shoved her into the tub. "My brothers told me—"

The rest was drowned out as they pushed her head under the water and yanked her back up again. "What was that, Dear?" Susannah asked.

"Are you bathing me—or trying to—drown me?" Tori sputtered between coughs. She clutched the sides of the tub for dear life, determined to battle if they tried to dunk her again.

"I do declare! I hope you have a good pair of scissors, Rach, because this hair is in an awful state."

Tori felt as though her skin was on fire as they scrubbed her arms and back. "My mind was more on these ragged hands of hers! It's going to take three months just to get them looking female again!"

"But did you see her—"

Their conversation was brought to a halt by an outraged screech. "Quit talking about me like I'm some old heifer you're lookin' ta butcher! I know I ain't nowheres near being a lady like y'all, but that don't mean I'm worthless! Why, toss a penny in the air, and I can shoot a hole clean through the middle of it. I can hunt and fish better than my brothers ever could, and I can run faster than deputies in five different counties!" As soon as she finished her speech, she closed her eyes and slumped down into the water, horrified she'd lost her temper with two ladies who only wanted to help her. Well, they surely wouldn't want to have anything to do with her now!

Her eyes flew back open the moment she heard Susannah laugh. "Honey child, we're not sizing you up to make you feel like a cow. We just need to get a measure on what all we need to do to turn you into a butterfly!"

Rachel smiled at her and started lathering her hair. "That's right, Tori. We're not taking away your abilities. We're just teaching you how to do other, more lady-like things."

Wincing at the not-so-gentle washing she was receiving, Tori mumbled, "I'm sorry I got so mad."

"Don't fret over it, Sugar. I'm sure we'll make you mad some more before all this is over with," Susannah replied pleasantly.

She lifted a pitcher of water from a small table and called out, "Close your eyes and hold your nose!"

Tori gasped as the tepid water rained over her head and shoulders.

As the evening wore on, Tori realized Susannah wasn't exaggerating. Yet, despite her inner urgings to lash out, Tori managed to hold her tongue.

The worst part came while they were eating dinner. Susannah had gone home, and Tori thought that only Rachel, her husband, and their four children would be in the dining room. Instead they were joined at a long table by seven more children and an elderly lady Rachel introduced as Gladys, the woman who managed the orphanage.

Set in the middle of all these people was dish after dish of the most delightful food Tori had ever seen or smelled. She quickly sat down and already had her hand on a chicken leg when Reverend Stone cleared his throat loudly and said to his eldest daughter, "Emmy, would you like to give thanks tonight?"

Tori looked around her and saw the children from the

orphanage looking at her and giggling. Embarrassed at her blunder, she slowly lifted her hand from the food and clasped it tightly in her lap.

When everyone bowed their heads, she did the same and listened as the young girl spoke a pretty prayer asking God to bless their food and thanking Him for their family and friends.

Tori wasn't totally ignorant about such religious things, but she didn't know all that much about them, either. She had a vague recollection of going to church as a child, but it wasn't something her brothers continued once they were on their own.

As she looked around at the sincere faces bowed in prayer, she figured God must be pretty important to these folks.

After everyone had said their "amens," Tori started to reach for the chicken. She caught Jessie, the Stones' oldest son, shaking his head at her from across the table, his eyes focused on hers. Without breaking his gaze, he lifted a bowl in front of him and in a slow, deliberate fashion, spooned the peas onto his plate, put the serving spoon back into the bowl, then passed it to his right.

Tori gave him a tentative smile as she picked up the platter of chicken and, using the large fork provided, carefully speared a piece and put it on her plate.

By the time the food was finally passed around, Tori was near to starving! It would probably be faster if everybody just grabbed their food and ate like she was aiming to do earlier, but apparently that wasn't the proper thing to do.

There were an awful lot of proper things that needed doing that she was urged to remember afterward. Don't talk with your mouth full, don't eat with your fingers, and a lady doesn't sop her bread in the gravy so that it dribbles down her chin when eaten!

Rules, rules, and more rules. How in the world was she going to remember them all?

She would, though. She was bound and determined to become a lady if for no other reason than to make that haughty sheriff eat his words!

Later that night, Tori realized the man would prove to be more difficult than she had first thought. When the rest of the family had long since gone to bed, he was still standing guard outside!

It was near midnight when Tori opened the curtain in her room for what must have been the fifth or sixth time, looked out, and again jerked the curtain closed because the sheriff was still out there! Didn't the man sleep? Was he going to stay out there, pacing back and forth, the whole night?

Blowing out a frustrated breath, Tori backed away from the window and walked to a fancy little table that was topped with a mirror. Rachel had called it a vanity. Settling into the chair in front of it, she studied herself in the mirror, noting the changes that had already taken place in just her first day. She was clean, for one thing, something she so seldom was from living on the dusty trail. She smelled sweet too, like wildflowers after a spring rain.

Rachel had done just as she'd threatened and cut off a great deal of Tori's hair. Although the length itself wasn't much shorter, she'd cut layers, making her hair more wavy and shinier than Tori had ever known it to be. She picked up the brush and thought about Rachel's instructions to brush it one hundred times before she went to bed. Of course, Rachel didn't stop to think Tori couldn't count past thirty or thereabouts. She had never had any need to count higher than that.

She did know how to read, however. Her oldest brother, Scott, had made sure of that. He'd been lugging around a satchel of books for as long as she could remember, not caring that it made traveling more difficult for him.

Tori understood why he did it, though. Reading gave her a chance to learn about things she normally wouldn't know and to live a charmed and adventurous life in her imagination.

She wondered if they allowed Scott to read in jail. She sure hoped they did.

Her other brother, Kyle, wasn't bookish like Scott, but he was a dreamer. It was usually Kyle who would map out their journeys and plan their pocket-picking escapades. He would constantly tell them that all they needed was to save a little of their money, and then they'd be able to buy a small spread of their own to raise cattle or to grow a good garden.

Poor Kyle just wasn't very good at handling their money. He'd end up gambling it away or throwing it away on something silly.

Well, she thought with a sigh, *reminiscing about them is just going to make me miss them all the more.*

Shaking off her melancholy thoughts, Tori stood and readjusted her robe. Resuming her inspection of her new self in the mirror, she took stock of her clothes. It didn't matter if it was daytime or nighttime, proper ladies wore a lot of layers that seemed entirely unnecessary. She'd always worn pants, not only to keep up her charade as a boy, but because it was easier to get around in boys' clothes than in dresses.

The starched nightgown, however, faded in her vision as she focused on the huge canopy bed in the center of the room and reflected in the background of the mirror.

No way was she going to be able to sleep in that thing! She'd lain down for all of two seconds before a choking feeling of panic swept over her. The lace curtains, which covered the whole thing, gave her a closed-in feeling. But even if it had been just a plain bed, she couldn't have tolerated the soft, feather mattress.

She was used to sleeping outdoors with nothing but a bedroll beneath her and the huge open sky above. And that's exactly where she planned on spending the night—just as soon as the nosy sheriff disappeared!

Walking over to the window, she drew back the curtain and glared at the man who stood leaning against a tree just outside the fenced-in yard. He wasn't even pretending to be out taking a stroll. Oh no. He was facing her window, just waiting for her to crawl out of it and escape.

Planting her hands on her hips for a moment, she stared back at the man who had been a constant irritation since he'd arrested her the night before. He seemed to grow uncomfortable with her gaze on him, and he looked away.

But only for a moment. He readjusted the rifle on his shoulder and resumed his surveillance.

She shook her head and swallowed the laughter bubbling in her throat. For some reason the whole situation struck her as funny.

Throwing up the sash, Tori leaned out the window. "If I

promise not to run away tonight, will you please go home?" she asked him in a loud whisper.

Now that she had a clearer view of Sheriff Billy, she could see the bags forming beneath his eyes and the weariness in his shoulders. The man was half asleep!

He stood a little straighter and fiddled with his hat, as if trying to assure her he was doing just fine. "Why should I take the word of an outlaw?" he asked in a low voice as he stared at her warily.

"Because this outlaw wants to go to bed but can't, knowing that you're standing out there glaring at my window."

He rubbed his face and seemed to think a moment. Finally he blew out a breath and nodded his head. "Alright. But I'll be back tomorrow," he warned.

"Never doubted it for a second, Lawman," she mumbled with a grimace as she slammed the window shut.

She watched as he lumbered down the street, rubbing his neck as he went.

She found herself smiling again but immediately stopped when she realized what she was doing. He was not a man to get friendly with, and she sure shouldn't be smiling at him!

Blocking him out of her mind, she began focusing on her immediate plans. Tori gathered the blanket from the foot of the bed and padded back to the window, hoping the Stones wouldn't catch her and think she was trying to escape!

four

In the month that followed, Billy Ray found himself ana-
lyzing and worrying over that little incident with Tori.
How could such an uncouth, uneducated outlaw make him
feel so many conflicting emotions all at once? She was
pretty, he'd have to give her that, and it wasn't just
because Susannah and Rachel had been dressing her. If
she wasn't such an insolent harridan he might even like
her—a little. But then again, even if she spoke the sweetest words this side of the Mississippi to him, it still would
do no good. She was an outlaw, and he was a lawman.

In his mind, the two just didn't mix.

Every night, he'd done just as he'd promised. First he
would watch as she walked the short distance from the
orphanage to the Stones' home, then drill Rachel and
Reverend Caleb on how her behavior had been that day.
He stopped staring at her window like he had the first
night because, well, it seemed to make her uncomfortable,
and he figured just thinking he might be watching her
would be enough to keep her indoors.

So far, she'd been a model citizen. But Billy Ray wasn't
giving up his watch totally. Sooner or later she was going
to resort to her old ways. When she did, he was going to
be there to catch her!

After Billy Ray finished locking up his office on this
particular Friday night, he started on his way to the Aaron

37

mansion, where he and his brothers all lived.

On a whim he decided to take one last pass by the Stones' residence.

He looked around the grounds, but nothing seemed out of the ordinary. The lights were out in the house, and the only sound came from the crickets hiding in the tall grass.

As he turned to leave, he saw something at the back of the house. He blinked and squinted his eyes to focus better in the blackness of the night.

Yep, something was moving all right. And unless coyotes had started walking on two legs, it had to be his outlaw!

With a satisfied smile curving his lips, he threw back his shoulders and drew his pistol.

He'd warned the judge this would happen. After all, a lawman is trained to know and sense these things.

With a cockiness he just couldn't seem to help, he started after his fugitive.

❧

Tori tiptoed silently out of the Stones' house, just as she now did every night, with her bedroll in her arms. She was learning to be a lady, slowly but surely, but she still couldn't get used to sleeping in a feather bed, all closed up within four walls.

She'd tried a couple of times but had ended up getting no sleep at all. So, when she was sure the Stones were asleep, she'd sneak out and make herself a pallet in the backyard just as she'd done the first night.

Tori suspected Rachel knew that she did this, but so far, she hadn't mentioned it. But that was Rachel. She had the ability to boss a person around like an army general and at the same time make them feel like they were the most special person in the world. Tori had felt as though she was part of the Stones' family from the very first day. Rachel and Susannah worked hard to teach her the genteel ways of being a woman, and though Tori felt silly learning how to hold a teacup or practicing how to say *isn't* instead of *ain't,* she appreciated it all the same.

What she didn't appreciate was how the overly suspicious sheriff kept such close tabs on her comings and goings. She couldn't even attend church without him glaring at her from across the congregation. He was just waiting for her to make a wrong move, to prove him right. But she wasn't going to give him the satisfaction! Even if she wanted to run, which she didn't, she would stick around just to get at him!

She found her usual spot under the big elm tree and was just about to drop her bedding on the soft grass when the click of a pistol stopped her cold in her tracks.

"You just hold it right there, Lady," he growled in a deep voice Tori was sure had frightened many a criminal.

But it didn't faze her.

Whirling around, she glared angrily at him. "What's your problem now?"

He aimed the weapon higher, at her face, as if she were having trouble understanding that he was holding a gun on her. "Be quiet! Now, just throw down the bundle you're carrying and get those hands in the air. And don't try anything stupid because I will shoot."

Tori could do nothing but stare at the stupid man for a minute. He was going to shoot her for sleeping outside? In all his snooping around, hadn't he noticed she'd done this almost every night?

But Tori was no dummy. He just might be crazy enough to shoot. She tossed the bedroll at his feet and threw her hands up with as much attitude as she could muster. Arching her brow, she spat out, "So what? Is there an ordinance against sleeping outside?"

"Give me awhile, and I'm sure I can find one." Billy Ray glanced down at the bundle, then back up at her. That's when he noticed what she was wearing. "You're wearing your nightclothes!" he charged with something akin to horror.

"Well, that's what a lady does when she's about to go to bed! Miss Rachel said so!"

"Nelson, you don't know nothing about being a lady if you think tromping around in the great outdoors in your nightclothes is proper!"

"Why you—you. . ." She stumbled on her outburst as she tried to think of a word to call him that wasn't on the list of words Rachel had told her she couldn't use. Coming up sadly empty, she said the first thing that popped into her mind. "You mean man!"

Her pause must have been too lengthy, for he was already bending down, shuffling one hand through the blankets. Of course he was diligent to keep the gun firmly trained on her.

"Find anything interesting?"

He stood, scowling. "There's nothing in there."

"I never said there was."

They stared at one another for a second, and Tori could tell his mind was whirling with confusion. "Can I put my hands down now? They're beginning to hurt."

His lips thinned in a grim line. "Not just yet!" She

sighed and tried not to think about them. "If you weren't stealing something, you must have been trying to escape," he surmised.

Clearly he isn't the brightest man in the world. "In my nightgown?" she asked sarcastically, hoping her expression said what she was thinking.

He let out a frustrated breath. "Then what are you doing sneaking around in the middle of the night?"

Her arms were really beginning to hurt. "I told you I was planning on sleeping out here! Can I please put my arms down?" she complained wearily.

He didn't seem to like it, but he nodded anyway and carefully uncocked his pistol. She breathed a little easier after the weapon was safely in its holster. Ignoring him, she immediately dropped down and began to straighten her bedroll.

"You ain't really going to sleep out here, are you?" he asked twice before she finally answered him.

"I believe I said I was—several times. Can a deaf man *be* a sheriff?"

"Ha, ha," he shot back as he bent down and grabbed the covers out of her hand.

"Hey! You—you. . ." She sputtered in frustration. "You give those back!" She yanked on the bedroll, but he was holding fast.

"I can't let you sleep out here, Nelson. Don't you know some unsavory man could find you out here and do you harm?"

They played tug-of-war for a moment before she gave up in a huff and glared at him. "A man like you, you mean? You *were* just threatening to shoot me!" He just stared back at her, refusing to take the bait, so she let her shoulders droop in defeat. "I've slept in worse places, Lawman. This place is like a castle compared to them."

The sheriff stared at her through the moonlit darkness, and Tori once again felt the funny fluttering near her heart.

"Did anyone ever hurt you?" His voice was unusually soft and filled with more concern than Tori expected from him.

She swallowed the lump that had formed, for reasons she couldn't fathom, in her throat. She'd not shed one tear in eleven years, but since meeting this man she'd cried more times than she could count. "No, not really. No one ever really figured out I was a girl, and my brothers kept me out of sight."

He nodded and asked another question. "Why are you sleeping outside when you have a safe place to sleep inside?"

She shrugged, trying to act nonchalant. "I feel like I can't breathe—much less sleep—in a small room surrounded by all that feather ticking and lace."

She expected him to laugh. She didn't expect him to step closer to her and place the bedding gently back in her arms!

Every bone in her body froze, and she discovered it wasn't just feather ticking that caused her to have trouble breathing! He hadn't even touched her!

She looked away, confused about the way he made her feel, and focused on what he'd just returned to her. "What—I mean, why. . . ?" she stammered as she struggled to understand what he was up to.

"I'm not a monster, Nelson," he interrupted gruffly. "Just don't leave this yard." He quickly turned and walked away.

Tori stared after him for more than a few minutes, clutching the bedding to her chest, trying to calm her racing heart. She almost hated that he had shown a different side of himself tonight. Before, she could resent and despise the man who'd arrested and humiliated her. Tonight, she couldn't even muster a little dislike.

Who was the real Billy Ray Aaron? The stern sheriff or the protective gentleman?

That was something she was going to have to think on this next week. Maybe she could talk to Rachel about it. No, she decided, that would be too embarrassing. Rachel would tell Susannah, and Susannah would want to discuss it in great depth and length. Something Tori tried to avoid!

But Rachel had also told her she could talk to God anytime and tell Him anything. So far, she hadn't really said much to Him. Part of her didn't really feel worthy to waste God's time talking about her silly feelings.

Reverend Caleb had said God loved everyone no matter what they'd done or how they'd been raised. He said that Tori Nelson was God's child and He loved her very much.

It was still sort of confusing to Tori, but she liked the fact that there was someone who thought of her as a daughter.

Coming to a decision, she quickly knelt down and clasped her hands under her chin, just as she'd seen Polly White do during the altar service every Sunday night at church. "Dear God," she began, "I know this is going to sound really silly to You, and if You have something else to do, like healing the sick or walking on the water, well, I will understand."

Peeking up at the sky, she decided He was listening and continued. "I'm a little confused about the sheriff. I know You must understand him, since I've been told that You created everybody, and I would dearly love for You to help me know how to deal with him. You see, sometimes he seems so cold and mean, I just want to rear back and hit him! But Rachel told me about the Golden Rule, so I know I shouldn't do that. Except, if the sheriff was following the Golden Rule, shouldn't he be treating me a whole lot better than what he's been doing?"

She sighed. "But, he was awfully sweet tonight. . . . You see my dilemma, God? He's just plain confusin', and I don't know what to do!"

Peeking out of one eye again, she looked up at the sky, wondering whether God was going to answer her now or later. Since there was no motion from above, she decided that this was going to be a "later."

"Well, that's about it." She finished with a yawn. She settled down in her bed and stared for a moment up at the stars.

"You know, I enjoyed our little talk. I think we should talk again tomorrow, if that's alright with You." She yawned again. "Oh! I almost forgot. Amen!" With that, she drifted off to sleep with a satisfied smile curving her mouth.

five

The first month proved to be nothing short of grueling to Tori, and all they did was focus on her grammar and grooming! She thought she'd never learn to speak the way Rachel and Susannah wanted her to, but slowly she began to correct herself when she said something the wrong way.

Tori had to watch herself, though! Susannah's drawn-out Southern accent and dialect began to slip from Tori's mouth. She asked Jessie one night if he'd pass the bread and then called him "Sugar." Everyone burst out laughing, and poor Jessie was beaming red with embarrassment.

The only time her speech seemed to resort to its former state was when she was dealing with the sheriff. He seemed to turn up everywhere she went, whether it was to church or town, his suspicious eyes watching her, just waiting for her to take off so he could throw her in jail.

And boy, was he hard to deal with. Losing her temper and spouting insults at him was almost a daily occurrence. Most of the time he'd retort that he was just doing his lawful duty, which just made her even angrier.

Tori often wondered if he'd been nicer before he'd become the sheriff, because everyone seemed to like him. Susannah would go on and on about how wonderful he was at the house and how he was so helpful to her, never minding to do his share like his brothers did. Rachel, too, would sing his praises, going on about how he donated so much of his time helping to find homes for their orphans. The wretched man even came over during the day to play with them. "He's going to make such a wonderful father some-day," was Susannah's favorite quote.

Maybe so, but he was failing miserably at being an over-seer of her sentence!

For some reason the man so annoyed her, she found her-self thinking about him every waking hour that she wasn't in some sort of lesson. At first she thought maybe he acted all high-and-mighty because the power of the office of sheriff had gone to his head. But when she finally went to Susannah's house, where Billy also lived, she realized he'd been raised believing he was superior because the Aarons were so rich!

Their three-story house was the closest thing to a palace Tori had ever seen. The floors were made of shiny marble she could actually see her reflection in. Huge crystal ceil-ing lamps that Susannah called "chandeliers" hung in every room of the house, and some even boasted two! The paintings hanging on the walls were what fascinated her the most. One of the hallways held portraits of Aarons dating back four generations. She couldn't help but think it must be nice to know who your great-great-grandfather was when she could barely remember her own father.

The richness of the Aaron home and land was so over-whelming that Tori thought she, too, might feel a little above the normal folk being raised in such a home as this.

But the more she thought of this particular theory, the more she knew it wasn't true. Sheriff Billy was as nice as pudding pie to everyone—but her!

Maybe it was because he thought she was a bad person.

What else could it be? She'd tried her best to be nice—well, maybe not her best, but the best she could to be civil to him. Then he would go and look down his nose at her or say something really superior sounding, and "nice" would just fly out the window.

It was just no use. She could learn to be the most genteel woman in Texas, and Sheriff Billy Ray Aaron wasn't going to see her in any way but as a worthless outlaw!

The second month went a little more smoothly, and thanks to having very few encounters with the sheriff, life was actually quite enjoyable. Oh, he was still around, but it was as if they had reached an unspoken agreement to simply not acknowledge each other.

Only, in her heart, she always knew he was in the room. He wouldn't have to speak, but she could always sense him nearby. And try as she may, she sometimes couldn't help but feel a little hurt that he was ignoring her, as she was him. A double standard, maybe, but there all the same.

Her comfort, however, began when she really started listening in church as Reverend Caleb preached his interesting sermons on Sunday. When they got home, she'd ask him questions about what she'd heard, and he never seemed to get tired of answering her.

Jesus wasn't a mysterious Being anymore as He'd once been, but now, thanks to Reverend Caleb, she had asked Him into her heart. To think someone loved her just as she was and that He would always be with her and never leave her was a miracle.

She hoped to one day be able to tell her brothers about the Christian life and what God could mean to them. She knew they could change and become respectable, law-abiding citizens with His help.

Tori was truly different now than when she first arrived in Springton, not only on the outside, but inside as well. She felt love from the Stones and *most* of the Aarons and felt so useful when she would help care for the children at the orphanage.

Her dreams finally seemed obtainable.

Or they would be if she managed to hold on to her dignity and sanity during the last month of learning about the law from Sheriff Aaron.

❧

Only one week to go. One week before he had to spend every day with. . .*her*. What was it about her that disturbed him so? He had dealt with some of the state's worst criminals and managed to keep a civil tongue, but every time he was around Tori Nelson, he'd bark like an angry bulldog!

He was normally a calm, rational man. He'd known what he wanted out of life at the age of fifteen and had set out to make that dream happen.

He loved everything about the law, probably because he was the type of person who wanted things neat and in order. Life was simply black-and-white, and where things seemed a little gray, there was a law to hopefully make it clear.

Except that with Tori Nelson, nothing made sense. He tried to think of her as a criminal with a lesson to be learned. He had, after all, seen with his own eyes what she was capable of! She could lift a precious bauble or coin off someone and never think twice about how it would affect that person. She'd been robbing and thieving all her life with the help of her reprobate brothers. In the eyes of the law, she deserved to pay for what she'd done!

But on the other hand, he knew in his heart she was a victim of her circumstances and her lifestyle was not of her own choosing. If her parents had lived, she might have had a normal upbringing, perhaps learning the same values and morals he himself had been reared to uphold. Susannah had filled him in on how bad it had been for her out on the trail, sometimes half starving, as her brothers tried everything they could to make sure she survived.

Billy had seen the vulnerable side of her, the side of her that worked so hard to be a lady and to do the things Susannah and Rachel were teaching her. The unbelievable thing was that her efforts were paying off. He'd watched as she blossomed like a flower, leaving little trace of the raggedy creature he'd arrested.

And this was his dilemma. On one hand she was a criminal and deserved to face punishment. On the other, she was a victim and deserved a second chance.

There was no black-and-white where Tori Nelson was concerned. No absolutes. No order. And certainly no peace.

He'd found himself staring up at his ceiling many a night, trying to comprehend and reason with himself about why she affected him the way she did.

Was it guilt over the way he had constantly snapped at her that first month? That was surely part of the reason. Maybe it was the frustrating fact that she didn't fit into the usual category where he put other criminals. He couldn't file her memory away and congratulate himself on a job well done as he'd done in the past.

It couldn't be because she was so pretty—as his brothers so frequently pointed out. And it sure couldn't be because her laugh seemed to sing straight to his heart or that her smile seemed to light a room the instant it appeared.

He wasn't some young greenhorn who'd let a pretty face sway him away from his duty!

To prove he had no attraction to her whatsoever, he had practically ignored her for the whole month. Only a handful of words had passed between them, and if it wasn't for the judge's order for her to learn something about the law from him, he would have gone on pretending to not take notice of her!

Of course, she didn't seem affected by his lack of attentions. In fact, she was doing a little ignoring of her own!

That really irritated him.

What it all boiled down to was that Tori Nelson was a walking contradiction his life could well do without.

He decided to start building a house, just to get his mind off things. Of course, his eldest brother, Bobby Joe, became unhinged when he learned that Billy wanted to move out on his own. He couldn't understand why Billy would want to live elsewhere when the Aaron mansion was big enough for several families to live in.

But Billy had always had his own ideas about things, and it just so happened that many of those ideas broke with the traditions of his family.

He wanted to build his own house on a particularly beautiful piece of Aaron land that sat high on one of the few hills in the area overlooking Springton. One day, he'd live there in peace and harmony with a sweet little wife and their three or four children.

A nice, orderly life.

He imagined for a moment what it would be like to have Tori for a wife and was dismayed to realize the idea wasn't as abhorrent as he thought it would be. He decided that dwelling on it was better left alone!

These conflicting sentiments were wearing him out. He had an office to run, a town to protect, and a house to build. He didn't have time to be worrying about this confusing outlaw woman! Sitting up in his heavy wooden desk chair, he tried to concentrate on a telegram that had just come through the wire about two escaped outlaws.

His concentration was shot the moment two of his brothers sauntered into the office.

"If this ain't the easiest job around, I don't know what is," Tommy drawled as he grabbed a chair, flipped it around, and sat, leaning his brawny arms across the back. "Ain't there some criminals you need to be arresting or something?"

Danny grabbed the other chair and sat down beside his brother. "Aw, Tommy. You know he has his hands full building a house—which Bobby Joe is still sore about, by the way—and watching the pretty prisoner who's staying with the preacher and his wife." He grinned conspiratorially at Tommy. "You know, the one that nearly chewed his arm in two."

Billy gave his brothers a bored look. Being the youngest, Billy was used to his older brothers giving him a hard time. "You two have a reason for coming down here and harassing me?"

Danny, the oldest of the three and the most charming of the Aaron clan, tipped his Stetson back, showing off his deep auburn hair. He gave his brother a shrewd look with those blue Aaron eyes. "Well, I just wanted to know what was wrong with you yesterday at church. You looked wound up tighter than a spool of barbed wire."

Tommy leaned closer. "We thought it might have something to do with Tori Nelson!" He winked at Danny. "We noticed she kept pretending *not* to look at you through the whole church service."

"And you, Mr. Rough-and-tough, sat in the pew like you couldn't move from the neck down. It seemed to me like you were doing everything you could to not turn in her direction!"

Irritated that they were correct in their observations, Billy scowled at them and stood up. "If y'all will excuse me, I've got more serious things to do than sit here and listen to your fairy tales!"

He stomped around them and out the door, hoping they'd go on about their business.

That hope was not to be realized.

"Hold on, Billy Ray, we'll come along and help," Danny said, his voice teasing and mischievous.

Billy rolled his eyes as his brothers walked on either side of him. "Did Bobby Joe fire you two? Is that why you have time on your hands?"

"Aw, Bobby Joe ain't even at the office. Susannah's got him roaming around by the creek picking blackberries," Tommy answered.

Billy Ray shook his head in mock sadness. "I remember a day when our big brother was all work and no play. Now he's lollygagging around in the middle of a workday. That, brothers, is the work of a woman!"

"He's turned into a lump of mushy dough, if you ask me. Ain't no way I'm going to let a woman turn me into a softy!" Danny declared just as two pretty ladies passed him, giving him flirtatious smiles.

He smiled back and winked, stumbling and stepping on Billy's foot in the process. Tommy and Billy glanced wryly at one another. "You can't even walk straight when women are around, Danny. Forget dough, you'll be butter all melted on the floor!" Billy said, laughing.

Danny straightened his shoulders and adjusted his hat. He opened his mouth to say something but then stopped. A big grin creased his face, and he pointed toward the bank. "Seems like some other fella may be the one melting. Look over yonder. Isn't that Rance talking to your pretty prisoner, Billy Ray?"

six

Billy Ray's gaze followed to where Danny was pointing, and sure enough, it was Tori standing there as pretty as she pleased talking to Rance Conway, the foreman of the Lucky Day Ranch. While Rance was a friend of theirs, he was also the biggest womanizer this side of the Mississippi! His good looks and cowboy charm were such that he even gave Danny a run for his money, but only a little. While Danny was an Aaron, therefore from one of the wealthiest families in Texas, Rance was just a poor ranch hand. When it came to serious marriage-minded mothers on the lookout for husbands for their daughters, Rance didn't even rank in the top ten.

But Tori didn't have a mother.

What she did have, though, was the Aaron and Stone clans watching over her.

He did, however, notice how close Rance was standing to Tori and how he reached out to kiss the back of her hand. He didn't miss the flush that swept over her face, either. The cowboy was dealing out the flattery, and she was soaking it up like a sponge.

What was she doing out alone? Either Rachel or Susannah was supposed to be with her at all times. Didn't they realize Tori was a child in many ways? She was versed on how to protect herself in a full-out attack, but she was not prepared for a subtle attack from men who didn't have her best interest at heart.

"Uh, Billy Ray? You alright?" Tommy asked.

"Yeah, you look a little hot under the collar. That wouldn't be jealousy, would it, Brother?" Danny teased.

Billy briefly threw his brothers a preoccupied glance before returning his attention to Tori and the cowboy. Without giving it much thought, he headed their way, determined to intervene.

He was stopped when his brothers jerked him back by the shoulders. "Whoa there, Sir Galahad! You ain't about to go make a fool of yourself, are you?"

Billy turned to Tommy in aggravation. "What do you mean?"

"He means if you go charging over there and fuss at Miss Nelson, you'll just embarrass her, Rance, and most definitely yourself," Danny answered.

Billy took a deep breath and tried to calm himself. His brothers were right. There wasn't any sense in making himself look foolish. But he did need to find out why she was out without an escort.

"You both know how Rance is; I don't want him thinking Victoria Nelson is easy pickin's."

Tommy snorted. "Aww, Rance is harmless. He's just looking for a wife is all. Maybe the two of them would be a good match."

"Tommy's right. Neither of them has a family, and he might be Miss Nelson's only chance at catching a husband. She did pick the pockets of most of Springton's well-to-dos," Daniel pointed out.

"She can just hold off finding matrimonial bliss until her sentence is over! I ain't got time to play chaperon while Tori courts every cowboy in the county!"

Tommy and Danny glanced meaningfully at one another at the use of her first name.

Billy shoved at both of them. "I mean Miss Nelson."

"I only see one cowboy she seems particularly interested in, don't you, Tommy?"

"One *very* interested cowboy."

Billy took a breath and tried to get hold of himself. "Look, whether it's one or twenty, she still shouldn't be out without a chaperon. Her escaping is all I'm concerned about."

"After two months of being a model citizen?" Danny actually laughed. "Keep talking, little brother. You might just start believing yourself."

"Regardless, I would suggest we go up to her, all friendly like, and politely ask if she needs an escort to the preacher's house," Tommy offered.

Billy nodded, and they started walking toward the couple. But the closer they got, the more irritated he became that she was out alone. How dare she put herself in such a vulnerable position! How could Susannah and Rachel fall through on their duties to watch out for her?

Tori looked up and met his gaze when they'd gotten closer. Only Billy knew why she instinctively took a step back, clutching her basket of daisies to her chest when she saw the annoyance radiating from his eyes.

"What are you doing out here without an escort?" he bellowed at her with all the irritation he was feeling.

Behind him, Tommy groaned. "Did you listen to anything we said, little brother?"

Danny added, "See! A woman can make a man go plumb crazy."

"What bee's crawled up in your bonnet, Aaron?" Rance drawled, as he stared curiously at his irate friend.

"Rance, I don't know what you think you're doing but—" Billy began to lash out but was stopped in midsentence when Danny jerked him back by his collar.

"Uh, he means he was concerned that Miss Nelson was unchaperoned, Rance. She's under his protection, you know," Danny hurriedly supplied.

"But I'm not—" Tori started to say.

"You don't have the sense of a lost goose, Woman! Didn't I just warn you about—"

"Now just hold on a minute, Billy. Where do you come from thinking you can talk to a lady like that?" Rance interrupted, his lazy smile transforming quickly into a scowl.

Billy opened his mouth to spew out more angry words, when he felt a nudge at his heart and mind, reminding him a wise man held his tongue when it had nothing good to say. He paused a minute and looked from his friend to Tori, who seemed to be waiting for more reprimands.

"You're right, Rance. I didn't mean to lose my temper. I was just worried that. . ." His words came to an abrupt halt. What exactly was he worried about? Worried she might escape when she'd shown no inclination to do so, or was he worried that she might enjoy Rance's flirtations too much? Was he. . .jealous?

Conscious of the odd direction his thoughts had taken, he noticed everyone staring at him and quickly dismissed the latter as crazy thinking. Of course he wasn't jealous! He'd have to like the woman for that, and he didn't make it a habit of going around befriending outlaws. Ridiculous!

"Worried about what, Sheriff?" Tori asked innocently.

Rance smirked. "I think he's just jealous that you're out here with me, Miss Nelson."

Tori surprised him by laughing. "Now that's the funniest thing I've heard all day! He hates me. Why would he be jealous?"

She turned her sparkling light blue eyes toward Billy as she spoke. He could read in them that she believed what she'd said, and that realization was like a blow to his chest. He hadn't realized that his actions were so harsh, his words so hateful. He was a sheriff with a duty, true, but he was also a Christian man with a bigger duty—to treat people with kindness.

He'd shown her anything but that.

"Miss Nelson, I don't hate you."

"You certainly don't like me much."

"I don't dislike you. I just have a job to do is all."

"Don't you need to get back to that job now?" Rance asked pointedly, as he stepped between them, breaking their intense stare.

"I am doing my job, Conway. Now if you don't mind, I still need to find out why either Rachel or Susannah isn't with her and—"

"Why, I'm right here, Sugar," Susannah interrupted as she, Bobby, and their daughter Beth walked out of the little shop next to the bank.

Because he'd allowed Rance to get to him again, his question came out a little harsher than he'd intended. "Susannah, why is Miss Nelson roaming around town by herself, unescorted?"

Susannah peered at her brother-in-law from behind her ever-present fan. "Billy Ray, Sugar, you are just going to have to calm down. The tiny little veins on your forehead are positively bulging."

"Now, Susannah, I need to know—"

"Relax, Billy Ray. She's been with us all morning," Bobby Joe scolded.

Tori pushed her way past Billy and Rance. "That's what I've been trying to tell him, but he wouldn't listen!"

Billy felt a little foolish for letting his tongue get away from him. But there was still one issue that had to be dealt with. "Susannah, you know the rules. You're supposed to be keeping an eye on her."

This time it was Rance Conway who spoke up, and his voice held just the tiniest bit of superiority. "I told her I would keep Miss Nelson company, Sheriff Aaron. Do you have a problem with that?"

The cowboy was beginning to get on his nerves. "Actually, I—" Billy began but was once again thwarted.

"Of course he doesn't," Tommy inserted firmly. "Do you, Billy Ray?"

"No," Billy answered tersely.

The air was thick with tension, but Billy just wasn't in the mood to make it any thinner.

So the ever-chipper Susannah did it for him. "Why, we had the most wonderful time searching for blackberries this morning, and you can see that Tori couldn't resist picking a basketful of the daisies she loves so much. We found so many berries, I had to purchase another basket to put them all in!"

"You're going to save some for us, aren't ya?" Danny asked hopefully.

"Only if you *all* behave yourselves and stop bothering

poor Tori!" She pranced over to Tori and took her arm, moving her away from the men. "We'll just be running along now. Toot-a-loo!"

Billy watched as Susannah, Beth, and Bobby walked away with Tori. But before they were gone, Rance had briefly managed to take Tori's hand again and say he'd see her at the church picnic later that week.

Billy Ray held on to his temper this time and managed to bite his tongue. Rance had never participated in a church social before, and he knew Rance was only doing it to get acquainted with Tori.

Billy had to tell Rachel and Susannah to talk to her about the men in town. She was pretty enough to make most men forget her shady background. Most men didn't care one way or another. But not all of them would be honorable in their attentions. In many ways, Tori was naïve when it came to men. He didn't want to see her get into trouble.

"Didn't anyone ever tell you, you can catch more flies with honey?" Danny asked, giving him a friendly slap on the back when they were out of earshot of the cowboy.

"You're going to need some self-control if you're going to keep dealing with Tori Nelson. You can't go around charging like a bull every time she does something that makes you mad."

"I know, Tommy. It's just—I can't think straight when it comes to her! I want to protect her and yell at her all at the same time," Billy declared, throwing his hands up in the air in a helpless gesture.

"Oh, no," Tommy and Danny groaned at the same time.

Billy turned and studied his brothers. "What?"

"She's gotten to you. You're a goner now," Tommy told him mournfully.

Billy scowled, swinging back around and trudging away from them. "You're crazy," he yelled over his shoulder. "She's just my prisoner, that's all."

"Maybe you're the prisoner, little brother," Billy heard Danny call out, followed by a round of male laughter.

Billy walked on, determined to ignore their taunt.

Or at least he tried.

seven

As Tori, Susannah, Beth, and Bobby walked past the sheriff's office, Susannah stopped and looked back. "Where did Billy go? I thought he was walking back this way."

Bobby shrugged and then nodded toward the stables that were past the bank. "No, look. He's over there talking to Harold Norton."

Tori's gaze followed to where Bobby was pointing, and at that moment, Billy just happened to turn and meet her gaze. Embarrassment at having been caught looking back at him, especially when he narrowed his eyes suspiciously, made her practically jump back around.

"What's wrong with Uncle Billy Ray?" Beth asked, glancing back and forth from her uncle to Tori. "Why is he frowning at us?"

"It's me he's glaring at," Tori answered. "I made him mad when he caught me alone with Rance."

"You know, I've never seen Billy act this way. He's usually so easygoing and charming." She peered over Tori's shoulder to take another look at her brother-in-law. "Why, he looks almost jeal—"

"Susannah!" Bobby warned while tugging on her arm. "Don't even say it."

Tori was confused. "He's almost what?"

Susannah started to answer. "I was going to say—"

"Nothing important," Bobby interjected firmly.

Tori shook her head. "But—"

"Uh, Tori, why don't you take a basket of berries to Billy's office?" Bobby interrupted as he took the basket of daisies Tori was holding and handed her the berries instead.

Tori looked down at the basket and then back up to Bobby and Susannah, who seemed to be having an argument without saying a word! Which was unusual in itself, considering that Susannah couldn't seem to do anything without talking!

Shrugging at Beth, who looked just as mystified as Tori felt, she let herself into the office.

A little shiver ran up her back as she glanced over to the jail cells. She hadn't been back in here since that first day, and she wished she hadn't come in here today. In a small West Texas town, her brothers were locked up in a cell like these. She prayed they were all right, that they were getting fed properly and treated well.

And because Tori was thinking about her brothers, she thought at first that she was dreaming when she saw her brothers' names on a piece of paper on the sheriff's desk. She put the basket down and picked up what she now saw was a telegram.

There in bold letters were the names Kyle and Scott Nelson, under which she read the words "escaped convicts" and a warning for the local sheriffs to be on the lookout!

Her brothers had escaped? Why would they risk so much when they were going to be released in just a few short years?

Something important must have happened to make them break out of jail. And if she knew her brothers, it must have something to do with her. Maybe they thought she was in danger or something.

Two years ago, when she'd told them she was leaving town, they'd put up a protest like she'd never seen. If they hadn't have been standing behind bars, Tori was sure they'd have chained her to them so she wouldn't go anywhere. But when she told them the rumor was going around town that a third boy had been with the brothers, they agreed she should go, especially before anyone found out she was a woman.

Before they suspected she might have the diamond.

That stupid, gaudy diamond was the reason for the whole ordeal!

Doogan McConnell had been wearing his trademark five-carat tiepin during a big shindig in the town square. Tori and her brothers had seen the party as a grand opportunity to do a little thieving since the whole town had been invited.

They had done pretty well with a few gold watches and a handful of coins and were on their way out of town when McConnell let out a yell. Every stranger in town was targeted and rounded up, all except Tori, who had managed to hide. But it was her brothers who turned up with items that weren't their own.

Though the diamond wasn't found on them, they were charged for stealing it along with the rest of the items.

Of course, McConnell believed they had hidden the diamond, and he promised that the moment they got out of jail, he was going to get it back one way or another.

McConnell wasn't a man who made threats he didn't keep.

Tori had been almost sure that no one connected her with her brothers, since she only came at night to speak to them from outside their barred window, but McConnell was smart and devious. He had spies camped out everywhere, and one of them had seen her speaking to her brothers.

That's when the rumors started flying and she knew she had to run. So, she had decided to head east. Although she'd come close to getting caught the first month, McConnell's men had not crossed her path in nearly two years.

That didn't mean they'd given up, though.

Now, her brothers were breaking out after two years. Why? Did they know McConnell was after her?

When she heard Susannah's voice call her from outside, she shook herself from her musings and quickly stuffed the telegram into her pocket. She didn't know if the sheriff had read it yet, but she was going to take it, just in case.

It would probably be awhile before her brothers tracked her down. She hoped and prayed the remaining four weeks of her sentence were over by then, because if not, she had the feeling her brothers would take her away from Springton to hide her from McConnell.

And then the sheriff would think he had been right about her all along.

❧

That evening, Tori, Rachel, and Susannah were sitting in Susannah's immense parlor as they patiently began to teach her how to embroider. But her mind was too occupied with other things to concentrate on the tiny stitches.

Tori's "other things" included contemplating her encounter with Rance Conway and mulling over the situation with her brothers. The two—on the surface—didn't have much to do with one another, but to Tori, they seemed directly connected.

In order to protect herself *and* find a way to help her brothers, Tori needed a husband!

She didn't know much about the way of things, but she did recognize that having a husband meant having protection. She'd listened as Rachel told her the story of how she and Reverend Caleb had fallen in love and how the town didn't accept her at first because she'd been raped and that a child had resulted from it. But once they learned the truth and she had married the preacher, well, it wasn't long before it was all forgotten and she became accepted.

Reverend Caleb had added that he would have married her even if the town had never accepted her because God had put them together. He also said that he loved her and would have simply moved to another part of the country to protect her.

Maybe God was working out something for her too. Maybe He was the one who gave her this marriage idea in the first place. And just maybe God had worked it out so that she and Rance Conway were in town at the very same time! Rachel often said God worked in mysterious ways! This seemed to be a little mysterious. . .didn't it?

Rance had seemed interested in her from the start. Tori may have played at being a boy all these years and not participated in regular conversation like a woman does with a man, but she was female enough to recognize flirting when she saw it!

Rance had come right out and told her he thought she was the prettiest "filly" he'd ever seen. Tori wasn't so sure she liked being called a horse, but he'd made it sound nice, so it must be a good thing.

"Tori?" She heard her name called. "I declare, Rachel! I believe our young friend looks a little dreamy tonight! I wonder if it could be because of that handsome cowboy she was talking to earlier in the day."

Tori's eyes widened and looked at Susannah's teasing face with surprise. "How did you know?" she blurted out, giving herself away. She instantly blushed and looked back down at her stitching.

"What cowboy?" Rachel asked with interest.

Susannah laughed. "Why, the foreman of the Lucky Day Ranch, Rance Conway! He stood with our charge outside of the weaver's shop as Bobby, Beth, and I went in to get a new basket."

"Susannah!" Rachel sounded slightly scornful. "You know we're not to leave her alone. Why, Billy would have had a fit if he knew this."

"Oh, he knows. And you're right—he absolutely came unhinged when he saw Mr. Conway with Tori. I, myself, think he was pure-de-old jealous!"

That statement brought Tori out of her embarrassment, and she couldn't stop the laughter that bubbled up from her lips.

"Now, that's exactly what Mr. Conway told him!" She put her embroidery hoop down and leaned back on the sofa. "But I told Billy Ray I knew he hated me. The sheriff would like nothing better than to see me thrown into jail and left there to rot."

"Now, that's about the dumbest thing I've ever heard," Billy spoke from the doorway of the parlor, causing all three ladies to jump in astonishment.

Tori could feel her face really burning with embarrassment this time. Why couldn't she just keep her big mouth shut?

The sheriff tossed his hat onto an empty chair and walked steadily toward her with a glint of determination and displeasure in his eyes. She wanted so badly to look down and run away from him, but the pride in her just wouldn't let her. No sir. If he could stare at her, she could just give him as good as he gave.

Billy stopped right in front of her, his long legs almost touching her knees. As he looked down, a lock of his shiny, light brown hair fell over his tanned brow, causing his face to take on a boyish look.

"Didn't we just settle this matter? I've never hated anyone in my life, Miss Nelson, and I certainly don't hate you." He waved his finger at her to make the point. "What you've seen is just me doing my—"

"If you say you're just doing your job again, I am going to hit you!" His superior tone was really making her mad! She stood up suddenly, placing her hands squarely on her hips, making him stumble back to give her room. "Because, you see, I don't believe you, Lawman! I've seen you arrest two men in these past two months and both times you treated them like they were guests in your jail hotel! You smile at them and sneer at me!"

"Maybe if you had cooperated like they did, instead of chomping on my arm and making me chase you all over town, you would get the same treatment."

"What's your excuse now? I haven't bitten you or tried to run away in two months, but you still treat me mean!"

"You know, she does have a point, Billy Ray. You do go

overboard on playing the big, bad sheriff when Tori's around," Susannah chimed in, making Billy step away from Tori and look toward his sister-in-law.

Tori realized she could suddenly breathe a lot easier now that he was not standing so close! Why, she was positively perspiring!

"Susannah, I have a job to do—"

Without giving it a second thought, Tori slapped his arm. "I warned him," she announced in her defense to the ladies.

"And he rightly deserved it too. I've wanted to do that very thing, only harder," Susannah replied, as she whipped out her fan and lazily began to swish it back and forth. "But let's get back to the point at hand here. As I was saying earlier, Billy, before you so rudely interrupted us, I thought you were almost acting like a jealous suitor when you saw Tori with Rance Conway today."

"Now—now, I'm just getting good and tired of—of hearing. . ." He sputtered to a stop, his face turning red with embarrassment.

"Oh, don't get all bent out of shape, Lawman. That's what started this whole thing. Remember?"

Billy looked back at her, his brow furrowed. "No, what started this whole thing was the fact that you were found unchaperoned with a man of questionable reputation! You're just trying to shift all the attention onto me by imagining that I'm jealous of you! Which is ludicrous, by the way!"

"I didn't say you were jealous!"

Rachel stepped up to them and gave them a placating smile that Tori didn't quite trust. "Of course you're not jealous, Billy Ray. We were just teasing you. Actually we were talking more about Rance Conway and what Tori thought about him."

Susannah was wearing an identical smile. "Why, yes! Tori had just admitted to us that she'd been thinking about him, didn't you, Tori?"

Tori knew then that whatever they were up to wasn't good. "I. . ." She didn't know how to answer! "I didn't exactly say that. . . ."

"Don't tell me you're sweet on Rance Conway!" Billy charged, his disgust written heavily on his features. "Don't let that cowboy turn your head. He'll flirt with anything wearing a skirt!"

All three women gasped, but it was Tori who recovered first, spurred on by her rising fury. "Just maybe it's him who's sweet on me! He even told me I was as pretty as a filly!"

Not a word sounded in the room as all seemed to wait with bated breath for Billy Ray to respond. He didn't say a word, though; he just looked at her like *that* was the dumbest thing he'd ever heard.

Tori looked over at Rachel. "It *is* a compliment, isn't it?" she asked, suddenly unsure.

Rachel smiled at Susannah and then blinked her eyes at Billy. "Why, I think that's the sweetest compliment a cowboy can give a girl, don't you, Billy Ray? You know how they treasure their horses."

He opened his mouth to say something but seemed to change his mind. Looking from one lady to the next, his gaze finally landing on Tori, he backed away a few steps and grabbed up his hat from the chair where he'd thrown it. "You know what, I'm going to leave you ladies to your sewing and get some fresh air." His gaze stayed on Tori for a moment, and she wished she could read his thoughts. The emotion flashing in his eyes was something she'd never seen before.

He looked away and nodded to the other ladies. "Y'all have a good night." With that, he left the room.

For a moment, no one said anything. Tori didn't think she was capable of talking because suddenly she felt like crying. Which didn't make a lick of sense to her!

She composed herself enough to look at Susannah and Rachel, who were staring at the door and smiling as though they were quite pleased about something.

Picking up her embroidery hoop, she plopped back down onto the sofa. Maybe her plan to marry Rance Conway wasn't such a good idea after all. It would obviously make Sheriff Billy mad and dislike her even more.

She didn't know why that bothered her, but it did.

eight

It was the Fourth of July, and the day of the picnic dawned. From the parsonage, Tori, Rachel, and Susannah could hear the townsfolk arriving, chattering and laughing as they entered the church grounds.

It was a fine day for a picnic. The birds were singing, the sun was shining, and there was just the slightest cool breeze in the air to keep the heat away.

The church grounds were decorated festively with red, white, and blue streamers laced from tree to tree. Table-cloths were draped over makeshift tables made of paneling and sawhorses, and tiny flags made by the women's quilting circle were placed on each corner for decoration.

Everyone was in high spirits and in a patriotic mood to celebrate their country's independence.

Why, then, did Tori feel like a cloud had descended over her head? Why wasn't she looking forward to the day like Susannah and Rachel?

Tori had a feeling it had something to do with the fact that the sheriff had gone back to ignoring her again. Yesterday he passed her on the street, nodded his head politely to Rachel, and pretended he didn't even see her. Tori had been the closest to him, and he'd just looked right past her.

Something sure had to be done before those law-teaching lessons took place. Unless he had found a way to teach her without talking or looking at her, he was just going to have to swallow his dislike and get along with her!

"You seem quiet, Tori. Aren't you excited about the church picnic?" Rachel asked as she pulled back the side of Tori's hair and started to fashion it into a loose bun in the back.

Tori shrugged as she handed a hairpin to Rachel. "I guess so. I'm just worried about a few things, I guess, and it sort of takes the fun out of the day."

"What are you worried about, Sugar?" Susannah asked, as she brushed out the wrinkles in Tori's new yellow skirt.

"I'm having mixed feelings about the men of this town. I mean, on one hand I'm flattered that Rance Conway seems to like me, but I'm not sure if I'd like him as a beau. Then there's Sheriff Aaron. . ." Her sentence ended with a heavy sigh.

Susannah looked at her with surprise. "What about Billy? He hasn't said anything else to hurt your feelings, has he?"

"That's just it! He hasn't said anything at all!"

The ladies were quiet for a moment, and Tori saw them exchange a glance. "And this bothers you?" Susannah finally asked, her voice casual.

Tori frowned. "Well, yeah—I mean, yes. I think if we're going to spend so much time with each other next week, we need to *at least* be civil." She stood and walked over to take the skirt from Susannah. "Ignoring me ain't being—I mean, isn't being civil."

"Yes, well, I see your point," Susannah answered slowly, throwing Rachel another look. "I'm sure he's just been busy. He told you himself that he likes you."

"Actually, his exact words were that he didn't *dislike* me."

Susannah shrugged and helped Tori into the skirt. "Oh, pooh. Men don't say what they mean, anyway. I'm sure he meant he likes you."

Tori wished with all her heart that it were true. It troubled her something fierce that Billy Ray Aaron didn't think much of her. For some reason, she wanted him to look at her with respect, to admit she'd changed for the better and that she wasn't the same person he'd arrested two months ago. Her feelings had certainly changed about him. Oh, she still thought he was a bit bossy and judgmental, but he was a good and honest lawman—one who truly cared about the town and the people in it.

Tori just wanted to be counted among those people.

"What about Rance, Tori?" Rachel asked as they straightened the puffed sleeves of her white, high-necked blouse. "Rumor has it, he's looking to settle down and marry. He seemed mighty interested in you when he stopped by yesterday."

Tori thought about sitting with Rance out on the front porch of Rachel's house just the day before. They had talked for thirty minutes or so, and he seemed like a nice and even charming gentleman. He would make some girl a good husband—she just didn't feel like it should be her, no matter how good the idea of marriage was.

"I do need to think about my future, don't I," she commented as she looked at herself in the oval mirror, thinking once again that she hardly recognized herself.

Rachel made a "tsking" noise and gently embraced the girl. "Sweetie, whether you settle down with Rance or not, you'll always have a place here with us. You are wonderful at working with the children, and we would be happy to have you stay on." She smiled at Tori's reflection. "A girl shouldn't have to marry just because there doesn't seem to be any choice."

Tori hugged Rachel and then turned to do the same to Susannah. These two women weren't much older than she, but they'd each been as close to a substitute mother as Tori had ever had. "Thank y'all for being so sweet to me. My brothers would sure be happy to know I ended up in such good hands."

"Aw, it's nothing, Sugar. You've been mighty brave putting up with all our doings! I honestly didn't think we'd accomplish so much in such a short time, but you happened to be a natural beauty on the outside and especially on the inside. That's what made the difference."

Rachel nodded to Susannah. "She's right, Tori. You really wanted to change, and now that you've got Jesus in your heart, you'll be different forever. And you'll never be alone, either. He'll be looking out for your very best."

Tori smiled at them both. Her spirits were boosted, and she was beginning to feel the dark cloud lift. "I think I'm ready to head out for that picnic now."

≈

Billy stood under the big elm tree out in the churchyard and found himself looking over at the preacher's house for what must have been the twentieth time. Realizing what he was doing, he jerked his head back around and tried to focus on the people entering the yard.

When he saw Rance enter the gate, he had to fight to keep the scowl off his features.

"Keeping the town safe, Sheriff?" Rance called out in a teasing tone, just as he had in the past. Apparently the incident in town the other day was forgotten.

Then again, maybe not. "Miss Nelson arrived yet?"

Billy bristled like a porcupine. "How should I know?"

"Because I know you've been watching the preacher's house. Figured you were waiting for her." He shrugged nonchalantly, but the glint in his eyes belied his innocent observation.

Billy straightened and tilted back his hat to better look Rance in the eyes. "Let's get it out in the open, Conway, right here and now. I need to know your intentions toward Victoria Nelson."

Rance narrowed his brown eyes and yanked his hands out of the back pockets of his jeans. "And what business would that be of yours?"

"She's my responsibility; you know that. And since I know your reputation is less than sterling when it comes to women, I need to know if your intentions are honorable!"

"About as honorable as you can get, Aaron. I plan on taking her for my wife!"

Billy, shocked to his toes by that statement, didn't say anything for a moment. "You want to marry her even though you know she's a convicted outlaw and known thief?"

Rance made a snorting sound. "You seem to be the only man in this town who has a problem getting past that! And besides, sending her to live with the preacher and his wife ain't exactly what I'd call 'convicted.' "

Blowing out a breath, Billy relaxed his tense stance.

"Then I wish you good luck. I hope you'll be happy," Billy told him with all the cheerfulness he could muster. Which didn't amount to much.

Rance shook his head and gave a half laugh. "Are you sure I'm not stepping in on your territory here? You don't look happy for me; you look like you want to deck me."

"You're crazy. How do you think it would look for the town sheriff to be courting the same woman that he'd arrested?"

"Not half as bad as you seem to think it would, Billy."

Billy stared at the cowboy for a moment. Rance's words were hitting him like blows to the chest, but there was no way he was going to let him know that. "Miss Nelson and I don't even get along, so it doesn't matter anyhow," he lied, knowing it did matter. More than he cared to admit.

"Then your hardheadedness is my gain." Rance glanced over to the parsonage. "Here she comes now." Billy followed Rance's line of sight to where Tori was coming out of the house. Her yellow and white attire made her look as pretty as the daisies that were pinned in her hair.

Rance tipped his hat to Billy. "See you around, Sheriff."

Billy turned and walked the other way, toward the Aaron land. He couldn't watch as Rance romanced his way into Tori's heart. Of course they were a good match. And sure, she would make Rance a good wife. But it didn't mean Billy wanted it to happen.

And Rance had hit the nail on the head when he told Billy that only he had a problem with Tori being an outlaw. *A former outlaw,* he amended. But no matter how attracted he was to her, it still was there in the back of his mind.

He was a sheriff, and she was a former thief. No matter

what Rance said, it was his duty to be a good example to his people.

He'd almost reached the sawmill when he heard footsteps running up behind him. He couldn't believe it when he turned and saw it was Tori.

She slowed down to a walk when she noticed he'd stopped, and Billy could feel his pulse increase the closer she got. His gaze took in everything about her—from the loose strands of shiny golden hair that were blowing about her rosy cheeks to the slim, feminine figure he'd once mistaken for a boy's. She had such a poised and graceful walk, it seemed hard to believe she hadn't learned it from childhood.

She was the only woman on this earth to have ever taken his breath away—and that was from just looking at her!—and he couldn't do a thing about it.

The unfairness of that made him react to her in his usual *charming* way.

He snapped.

"You're without a chaperon again," he objected, a little harsher than he meant to.

"If you'll notice, Sheriff Aaron, I was running to you and not away from you," she pointed out matter-of-factly, seemingly not put off at all by his surly manner.

Feeling a little ridiculous for letting his temper get the best of him, Billy calmed down and tried to speak normally. "Did you need me for anything?"

"Wait a minute. Are you actually talking to me?" she gasped in mock wonder, dramatically putting her hand to her throat. "You walked right past me yesterday, and I was certain you had trouble seeing and speaking."

"Oh, I saw you, alright. I just figured if I pretended not to, we wouldn't have to argue," he returned pointedly, motioning with his hands that the present conversation proved his point.

A sheepish expression crossed her features as she looked away from him. "So, uh, why were you leaving the picnic?"

Suppressing a grin at her fast change of subject, he had to admire her intelligence and wit. Victoria Nelson was no dummy. Nor was she like most females he knew who wouldn't dare come right out and say what was on their mind. But Tori didn't seem to think twice about it. It was just one more item to reluctantly add to his list of things he admired about her.

She was waiting for an answer to her question, however, and it was one he couldn't answer with total truth. "There's still a little time before everyone eats so I thought I'd check on my house. It's still being built," he added awkwardly.

Her interest was clearly written on her face. "You're building a house?"

He nodded. "Right up there on the hill," he told her, pointing to the right of the sawmill.

"I see the frame!" The smile she bestowed upon him was like the sun peeking out after a rainy spell. "You're going to be able to see the whole town once it's finished."

A wild idea ran through his brain, and he voiced it before he could talk himself out of it. "You want to see it?"

Tori gave him a wide, encouraged smile that quickly faded into regret. "I can't. I told Rachel I would be right back. I think Mr. Conway wanted to talk to me about something."

Billy gritted his teeth so hard his jaw began to hurt. "Then you'd better hurry back."

"Before I go, I wanted to ask you a favor," she told him, putting a dainty hand on his arm.

He took a deep breath and tried not to concentrate on her touch. "What do you need?"

She withdrew her hand and nervously gripped her small purse. "I would like for us to try to be friends," she blurted out.

Mystified by this turn of events, he simply asked, "Why?"

He watched her swallow. "This coming Monday, we're going to be spending a lot of time with each other. I just don't think I can take arguing with you every day like we have been doing." She began to pace back and forth in front of him. "I know you don't like me very well, but I think if we both tried really hard, we could at least be civil."

"Alright."

"I mean, we're both adults. And as Susannah is always pointing out, adults should always, at least, try to get along."

"Miss Nelson, I said okay."

"If we can. . ." She stopped and looked at him. "You did?"

He grinned at her surprised expression. "I did."

"Oh! Well—then—that's good," she stammered. "I guess I'll see you later!" She backed away and waved at him. "Bye, Sheriff."

Billy waved back as Tori spun around and headed back to the church.

He was almost to his house when he realized that he

hadn't told her he actually *did* like her.

Then again, under the circumstances, it was best he kept that to himself.

nine

It was Monday morning, and the dreaded day to begin her
law lessons with the sheriff had arrived. As Tori walked
along the wooden planks of the boardwalk, her mind was
swirling with all the complications her life had recently
taken on.

Things were so simple when she was living and traveling around with her brothers. There was no etiquette to
worry about, no manners to mind, no grammar to correct,
and certainly no men to worry over!

Oh, her brothers didn't count. They were happy as long
as they were able to eat and find a nice place to sleep.

But ever since she'd met the sheriff, or rather been
arrested by the lawman, her life had been anything but
simple. Any other sheriff would have just arrested her,
taken her to the judge, and that would be that.

Billy Ray Aaron had seemed overly irritated from the
first about the fact she was a female outlaw. Maybe it was
because she'd bitten him—Tori didn't really know.

To make matters worse, then she began to like the man!
She, a thief and outlaw, was attracted to a hard-hearted
sheriff.

Why couldn't she fall in love with Rance Conway? He
had stayed by her side the entire picnic and had come right
out and asked if he could come calling on her sometime.

Tori had said "sure" because she didn't really know

what "calling" meant. Later, though, Rachel informed her that she'd agreed to let Rance court her!

Her first thought was to tell Rance that she really didn't want him to court her—she didn't like him in that way, but something stopped her. Maybe it was the dream she'd always had of being a wife and mother. With Rance, it was possible.

She would be a fool to throw that away—wouldn't she?

Approaching the sheriff's office, Tori hesitated for a moment and closed her eyes. Taking a deep breath, she prayed that God would help her get along with Sheriff Billy. She'd just heard Sunday's sermon about calling on the Lord in the time of trouble. Seeing as she felt trouble every time she got around the sheriff, she was going to be calling on Him a lot!

Of course he *would* catch her like that—her eyes closed and standing outside his door like she didn't know what else to do!

"What in the world are you doing?"

Tori opened her eyes and smiled at him like she didn't have a clue as to what he was asking. "What do you mean?"

He opened his mouth, closed it again, and frowned—a gesture she'd seen him do more than once. He finally shook his head and muttered, "Never mind."

Billy motioned for her to step into the office and then poked his head out the door once she'd passed. "Where's Rachel?"

She sat down in the chair in front of his desk and started pulling off the white gloves Rachel had insisted she wear. Honestly, gloves didn't make a bit of sense, seeing it was nearly ninety degrees outside! "She's at home," she answered nonchalantly as she turned her head to him, giving him a smile.

His frowned deepened into a scowl. "But—"

"She trusts me, Sheriff Aaron. I'm here, ain't—I mean, aren't I?" She jerked back around and sighed. "I thought we were going to try to be friends." Remembering to mind her manners *and* her grammar was going to be a real chore if he was going to keep being this ornery.

She heard the sheriff let out a loud breath as he walked around her and sat down at his desk. He shifted through a stack of papers, then picked one from the top. "I don't suppose you know how to read," he grumbled, peering over the paper at her.

Tori had to bite her tongue to keep from telling him exactly what she thought of his smug attitude. Instead she plastered on another smile, one Susannah insisted worked in all situations, and said, "As a matter of fact, I do, Sheriff Aaron."

"How?" he blurted with surprise.

The smile was getting harder to maintain. "Oh, you know. First, I started with my ABC's, then I—"

"I meant, how did Susannah teach you in such a short time?"

The smile disappeared. It took too much effort. "My brother Scott taught me. I guess we're not quite so backward as you thought."

He frowned. "Aw, I didn't mean it that way; I just didn't. . ." His voice trailed off as he searched to come up with an explanation.

"Think?" she supplied helpfully. Billy jerked his head up, and as soon as their eyes met, they both started to chuckle.

"Something like that," he admitted, his smile still lingering on his ruggedly handsome face.

He turned his attention to the papers once again. "I guess we can start with me explaining about the U.S. justice system. Actually, from all I've read about other countries, I believe the United States has the fairest laws and the most organized court system in the world. In fact—"

He came to a halt when he heard Tori make a snorting sound. She just couldn't seem to help it.

Arching an eyebrow, he asked, "Is there a problem, Miss Nelson?"

She tapped her fingers on the arm of the chair. "It's nothing."

"It's obviously something, or you wouldn't have interrupted me. So, out with it."

Tori shrugged. "It's just that if the U.S. has such a fair and honest justice system, then why do so many crooks get away with their crimes?"

She could tell she was irritating him again since the muscles in his jaw seemed to be in a clinch. "Like you and your brothers did for—how many years have you been a thief?"

She ignored his sarcasm. "That's just what I mean. It's the folks like us who get caught, not the rich ones. Why, I've seen more bigwigs in town rob people blind with crooked dealings and then pay off the lawmen so they'll look the other way." *Like that varmint Doogan McConnell!* She wouldn't be surprised to learn he'd acquired his diamond by stealing it himself, in the first place!

"Well, those are the exceptions to the rule." When she

tried to refute that, he continued, *"But* it doesn't mean our courts are all failures! The majority of cases tried are done fairly and justly."

"But you didn't think my sentence was fair or just, did you?" She couldn't help goading him. It was still a sore spot to her.

He raked a hand through his hair. "No, I guess I didn't at the time, but now I think it was for the best."

Tori sat there stunned that he'd admitted such a thing, and once it was out of his mouth, the sheriff looked equally stunned! "But the law's the law, you said," she commented after a moment.

He fiddled with the papers in his hand. "Yeah, well, some things aren't always as cut-and-dried as I expect them to be."

What was this? The high-and-mighty lawman admitting he was wrong? Why did he have to break down and tell her this? It was the one thing that kept her from totally liking him. The fact that she thought he wanted her in jail helped make the attraction she felt for him easier to deal with.

A strange silence blanketed the room as they both considered each other and what had just been said. It was almost as if there were an expectancy for more to be said, yet a fear to say any more.

"Anyway," he mumbled, as he moved his gaze from hers and back down to his paper. Disappointed, Tori looked down at her gloves, which she had just unknowingly crushed.

For a half hour, Sheriff Billy read from what sounded like a manual on the justice system at a speed faster than she'd ever heard. He seemed anxious to get the lesson over with as he zipped through one page and then another like a man on a racehorse galloping toward the finish line.

She couldn't understand a word he said—but it didn't really matter since her mind wasn't on the lesson. She spent her time admiring the waves of his short, light brown hair and the way his lips formed the words as he sped through them. Her brothers were tall, broad men, but she didn't think their shoulders compared to the manliness of Billy's wide, strong ones. His hands were nice too, she noted as they gripped the paper and occasionally pulled at his collar as if it were too tight.

It wasn't that he was the best-looking man she'd ever seen. His brother Danny was far more handsome, and so was Rance for that matter, but there were qualities about Billy that appealed to her—he was strong, capable, and self-assured. A man who took his responsibilities seriously. A man who could admit he was wrong, on occasion.

Still, he was also the man who had arrested her and one who'd do so again in a second if he suspected her of further wrongdoing.

If only her heart fluttered for Rance the way it did for this lawman.

"So, do you have any questions?"

Tori blinked and pulled her mind back from her musings. "What do you mean?"

He looked irritated again. "Did you even listen?" He shook his head. "Is there anything you want to know about what we've gone over today?"

"Just one thing," she answered. "Is the law always as boring as this?"

He slammed the papers down on the desk. "I am not

doing this to amuse you, Miss Nelson, but to teach you right from wrong."

She fanned her gloves back and forth. "Well, the preacher does the same thing on Sunday, but he's a whole lot more interesting."

Susannah was right. There actually was a little vein that throbbed on his forehead when he got mad.

"Are you deliberately trying to goad me?" he charged.

She took a breath, feeling kind of ashamed, but only a little. "I just don't see how you can enjoy a job like this where everything is full of rules and regulations! Don't you ever have any fun?"

"Of course I have fun. I have fun every day!"

She looked at him in disbelief. "Doing what? Everywhere I see you, whether it's at a social or on the street, you are always wearing that badge and making sure everything is alright with everyone."

He leaned back in his chair and crossed his arms. "My job is fun, Nelson. I like being the sheriff. It's all I've ever wanted."

Tori watched as he turned pink at having admitted something so personal. "Well. . . ," she floundered, not wanting to embarrass him more but still wanting to get her point across. "I just think there's more to life than making sure everybody is living theirs by the law."

He studied her for a moment, making her own face redden a little under the scrutiny. "What about you, Nelson? What do you plan to do now that your thieving days are over?"

"Well, I'm not going to go back to it, if that's what you're getting at!"

"It never entered my mind."

"Thieving wasn't fun; it was a necessity—the only way I knew how to eat!"

"But you know now that you don't have to be a thief to survive."

"That's right. I have. . ." *Now, what was the word Rachel used? Oh!* "Options. I have options!"

He narrowed his eyes on her. "I suppose Rance Conway figures into these options?"

Tori maintained a blank face, though her hands were crushing her poor gloves again. "Maybe."

He was the one who let out a disbelieving snort this time. "I know good and well you agreed to let him call on you."

She gasped. "How—"

"Oh, he told me himself. Took great pleasure in it too, since he thinks I might want to call on you myself."

She would not let him see how his words affected her! Thrusting her chin into the air, she retorted, "Well, I'm sure you told him it was a ridiculous thought."

"You bet I did."

She blinked a couple of times. "Sure you did." Her voice drifted off to a choking whisper, and she immediately cleared her throat.

Tori finally looked up to find him studying her again. "I'm sure you feel the same. After all, I *am* the man who arrested you and threw you in jail."

She nodded. "Of course I feel the same."

"Of course," he muttered with a frown, as if that wasn't what he expected to hear.

What did he want her to say? That she wanted him to like her? That she wished Billy would tell Rance to stop wasting his time, that he wanted to court her?

It would never happen. To him, she'd always be a thief. Someone beneath his contempt.

"Anyway, why don't you take these home, and we'll discuss them tomorrow." He held out a couple of papers and when she reached out to take them, their hands touched.

Tori, startled, lifted her gaze to his, but he quickly looked away and shoved the papers toward her as if they were burning his hand.

She clutched the papers to her as she stood up. "I'd better go."

Billy stood also and nodded. "I guess I'll see you tomorrow."

Biting her bottom lip, she nodded and quickly left the office and ran down the street. Tears were threatening to spill from her eyes, but she sniffed them back.

Nelsons didn't boo-hoo like babies, her brothers had always told her, unless it was something worth crying over. Letting herself get all upset by the sheriff's thoughtless comments didn't seem worth her time. Nothing was going to change by crying over him. He was who he was, and she was who she was.

There just didn't seem to be a middle ground for them to meet on.

She took several deep breaths and smoothed her hair back from her face. She slowed her steps when she neared the large window of the mercantile.

The doll was still in the window—the same doll that had caused her to be arrested because she'd not been able to resist taking a look at it. The doll had given her a whole new life.

A feeling of peace poured over her heart and mind as she stared at the pretty toy. She knew it was the workings of God that put the doll right in the window so she could see it that day two months ago. Otherwise, she'd still be on the run, still be living on the streets, and still be a thief.

There would have been no friends, no helpful lessons on how to become a lady, and no relationship with God.

For the first time, she said a prayer of thanks for allowing her arrest to happen. She had felt like her world had come to an end that day, but God had managed to turn her circumstance around. God had given her a whole new world instead.

ten

"Miss Nelson, can you please sit so we can discuss the laws you read last night?" Billy asked for the second time as he watched her roam around his office. She was dressed all in green this morning with matching ribbons strung through the curls on top of her head. It was a complicated hair arrangement, and Billy idly wondered why womenfolk went to so much trouble on such things.

Tori picked up a rock he had set on his desk. "What's this for?" she asked curiously, examining it closely.

Billy gritted his teeth to keep from yelling at her. "I use it to hold down my papers. Now, can we get to the les—"

"Why don't you just put them in your desk?"

"Because I want them on *top* of my desk," he stressed tightly.

She examined the rock again, shrugged, causing her puffy sleeves to touch her cheeks, and then put it back on his desk. Walking over to the window, she pulled the plain, blue curtain back and peered out.

"Miss Nelson, can you please—"

"Can't you just call me Tori?" she interrupted as she whirled around, causing her dress to fan out around her.

She looked so pretty standing there with the sunlight streaming in—he would have liked to tell her he would do anything she liked, but prudence prevailed.

"It's not proper."

She made a growling noise to show her irritation, he supposed, but finally came over and plopped down in her chair for the first time that day. "I just don't understand some of the fuss you people make over what's proper and what ain't—I mean, isn't," she corrected with a grimace. "What does it matter if I call you Billy and you call me Tori? We'd sure save a lot of talkin' leaving off 'miss' and 'sheriff.' "

Billy put his hand over his mouth to cover his smile. She pointed out things most folks had thought about but never thought to voice. "It's just the way it is," he answered.

"And that's another thing!" she cried as she jumped up and began pacing back and forth. "Why is it the way it is? Did someone sit down and write rules on what was right and what wasn't? If so, I wish I had the book so I could remember all I'm supposed to!"

Billy laughed. He just couldn't help it. Victoria Nelson could be a real hoot!

"What's so funny?" she demanded, putting her hands on her hips and glaring at him.

He tried to stifle his laugh as he shook his head. "It's just that you worry about the silliest things."

She surprised him by suddenly smiling. "See? That's what I've been trying to tell you! It's all just a bunch of silly nonsense."

A smart man knew when it was time to give in. "I'm agreeing with you. Now, can you please sit down so we can get started?"

Surprisingly, she did as he asked, but that didn't mean she was going to be cooperative. She took the papers she'd folded up in her purse and slapped them dramatically on his desk.

"Speaking of silly. . ." She let her words drift off with a meaningful glance and motioned toward the papers the laws were written on.

He groaned and ran a weary hand across his face. "What could you possibly find silly about the law?"

She rolled her eyes at him and grabbed the papers back up. After a brief scan, she handed the top one back, pointing to a specific law. "That one. It says that it is illegal to shoot a buffalo from the second story of a hotel."

Billy frowned and snatched the paper to look at it closer. "I'm sure that's there because some folks were getting out of hand and shooting up all the buffalo," he defended lamely.

She shook her head as if he were dense. "How would this help? Couldn't they just go down to the first floor and shoot them? Why just the second floor? That don't make a lick of sense!"

"It don't need to make sense. You just need to obey it!" he blurted out, knowing he wasn't making any sense himself. How she managed to get him so out of sorts was beyond his reasoning. "I mean, I'm sure there were reasons for making it a law, but I just don't happen to know them right now."

She read from the second paper. "How about this one: 'When two trains meet each other at a railroad crossing, each shall come to a full stop, and neither shall proceed until the other has gone.' " She looked up. "How can one go if both of them have to wait for the other?"

This wasn't what he'd had in mind when he thought about teaching her the law! "Miss Nelson, can we just get to the laws that may apply to you someday? How about the ones on stealing another's property? Did that one ring any of your bells?"

"How's a person supposed to know all these silly ones, though? What if I do something like go barefoot down the street? I could be arrested and not even have a clue that I was doing something wrong!"

"Nelson, you can't be arrested for going barefoot!"

She had a superior look as she handed him the third sheet of paper. "Oh yes, you can! Look at the one on the bottom of the page. It states that a person cannot go barefoot without first obtaining a special five-dollar permit."

Frowning, Billy looked at the paper, and sure enough, it was listed. Tired of having to defend his state's laws, he tossed it aside. "Look, Miss Nelson. I don't know one sheriff who would enforce this, but—"

"Then why is it there?"

"I don't know!" He practically yelled at her before he could stop himself. He cleared his throat. "I mean, it is another one of those laws that meant something at the time it was written; however, if we can get back to the laws that do make sense to you. . . ."

His sentence drifted away when Tori rounded his desk, took him by the hand, and pulled him out of his chair. Dragging him over to the window, she declared, "Now just look how pretty it is out there. Do you really want to discuss any more of this law stuff with weather like this just waiting for us?"

Billy, who had trouble thinking about the question with her holding his hand, did the only thing he could do to preserve his sanity. He pulled his hand from hers, yanked out a hanky, and mopped the beads of sweat off his forehead.

He couldn't believe it when she grabbed his hand once again and began patting it. "Sheriff? Why don't we do the lesson outside? You look like you could use the fresh air."

For an insane moment, he held fast to her small hand, reveling in the softness of her palm and the way it seemed to fit so nicely into his own. He found himself looking down at her, their eyes searching as if they were each trying to read what the other was thinking.

Swallowing hard, Billy had to fight the urge to just bend down and kiss her. Oh, but he wanted to. He wanted to forget his self-imposed guidelines and tell Rance Conway to go jump in the lake, that he would be doing the courting from now on.

Was she moving closer to him? Did she want him to kiss her?

"Hold still, Sheriff. You've got an eyelash on your cheek." Billy stood frozen as she leaned closer to him and reached up to brush the lash from his face.

He was losing his mind *and* good sense! Remembering to breathe, he stepped back from her and reluctantly let go of her hand. "Uh, thanks," he muttered.

She looked up at him with expectancy. "So, can we?"

He swallowed. "Can we what?"

She let out a breath and again looked at him as though he were dense. "Can we go outside to do our lesson? Are you alright?"

She started to reach up and feel his forehead, but he quickly stepped out of her reach. "Didn't Susannah and Rachel tell you it was improper to be touching a man who's not related to you?"

"They only said something like that when they were

lecturing me on being courted by Rance. We aren't court-ing, so I didn't think it mattered."

He frowned when she brought up the cowboy. "You bet-ter not let him touch you, either! Why I'll knock him into the next county if he tries anything, and you can tell him I said so!" he charged, getting louder with each word.

Tori stood staring at him with a gaping mouth. She finally asked him, "You're not mad at me again, are you? Because every time I bring up Rance you seem to get mad."

"I'm not mad," he bellowed, and then realizing his vol-ume, he calmed himself down. "You're my prisoner, and I'm just watching after you." He said it to remind himself as much as Tori. But when he saw the hurt in her face, he wished he'd kept his mouth shut.

"I am more than just a prisoner, Sheriff, just like you're more than just a keeper of the law. The difference is that I'm aware of it." The hurt pride in her voice shook him to the bone as she turned away from him and walked over to his desk. "I don't think I feel like more lessons today. I'll just take these papers home and read them again."

He watched her walk toward the door, and he ran to stop her. "Listen, Tori, I—"

"Bye, *Sheriff* Aaron," she pronounced pointedly, mak-ing it known she heard him call out her first name.

The door closed behind her with a slam, and Billy put both hands on the door, thumping his head on it a couple of times in frustration.

Turning and resting against the hard wood, he looked up and prayed to God, "Dear Lord, I'm trying my best to get along with Tori Nelson, but I seem to keep messing everything up. I want to do the right thing here. I want to teach her what I'm supposed to so we can both get on with our lives.

"I don't know why I can't seem to say the right things or do what's fitting when it comes to her. I see how wrong I was about her before, and I know she's special. Can You help me just get through this month? I really need Your help." He closed his eyes for a moment and then pushed himself up. "And please, help me sort out all these conflicting feelings I have about her too."

He walked to the desk and touched the rock that had so enthralled Tori earlier. Then, with a heavy, heartfelt sigh, he withdrew his hand and slumped down onto his chair.

❧

Tori's mind was reeling as she replayed the conversation she'd had with the sheriff. Why did she always have to get defensive? And why did Billy Aaron have to say things to make her defensive?

It gave her a headache just pondering over that one—which was why she wasn't watching where she was going, causing her to run straight into someone.

"Hey, watch it there, Lady! You almost ran me over!" a gruff voice exclaimed, just as she made contact with a big belly.

"Oh!" Tori cried, quickly backing up a few inches. Her eyes lifted to the man, and every bone in her body froze with shock.

Doogan McConnell stood before her. Except for a few less hairs on his balding head and a few more inches around his rotund waist, he looked just as she remembered him.

Tori had been in situations before where she'd gotten

out of jams using her calm, cool wit and clear thinking. Thankfully, those gifts didn't fail her today, either.

She made herself breathe, forcing her body to relax and keeping her face pleasantly blank. Over and over, in her mind, she kept thinking, *he's not looking for a woman—he's looking for a boy. . . .*

McConnell peered down at her, yanking his leather-studded vest straight and moving his cigar from one side of his mouth to the other. His expression suddenly changed from irritated to admiring as his gaze roamed down her figure.

His leer left Tori feeling dirty, and she wanted nothing more than to slap that smug smile off his face.

Thrusting her chin into the air, she picked up her skirts and tried to go around the man, but her move was thwarted when his chubby hand grasped her arm.

"Hold on a minute, pretty girl. What's your big hurry?" McConnell breathed in her ear so close she could smell his breath made rank from the cigar.

"Unhand me, you—Sir," she quickly covered. Her first reaction was to revert back to her old ways, to light into him as she had done others in her past. However, something stopped her. And Tori knew it was the Holy Spirit reminding her she was a Christian now. Reverend Caleb had told her such a thing would happen when she was about to make a wrong choice.

"I just want ta ask you a question, that's all."

She managed to pull her arm away and back up from him. Smoothing the sleeve of her dress, she asked, "What kind of question?"

He chuckled in an untrustworthy sort of way. "Not the

kind I would like to ask, I assure you." His insinuations were making her ill. "No, I'm looking for someone. A boy around sixteen or seventeen. Slim, dirty blond hair, probably dressed in ragged clothes. He was last seen wearing a leather coat with a lot of fringe hanging off it."

Tori was glad she'd gotten rid of that coat before she'd arrived in Springton. "You know, I think there was a boy who came through here fitting that description," she said slowly, with mock thoughtfulness.

His eyes lit up with greed. "You did? Do you know where I can find him?"

She swallowed and forced herself to remain calm. "I'm sorry, Sir. But the boy is no longer here in Springton. He left and hasn't been seen in two months."

McConnell spat out a curse word and didn't even have the decency to apologize for it. "Do you know where he might have gone?"

"I don't have a clue, Sir. Now, if you'll excuse me, I'm needed at home."

He barely glanced at her as he nodded his head. His thoughts were clearly on figuring out where he would look next.

Hiding her smile, Tori picked up her skirts again and walked around him, this time with success. When she came to the end of the sidewalk, she quickly ducked into the alleyway between two buildings and peeked back to where McConnell was.

A tall, mean-looking man she recognized as a fellow named Vega came up to him, and they spoke for a few moments. Then, to her horror, he stopped a couple of other folks walking by and spoke to them too. Tori knew he was asking them the same question.

She prayed no one would make the connection.

Each time, Tori saw the person's head shake in a negative response, and each time, she gave thanks to God.

After what seemed like hours instead of minutes, McConnell and Vega finally walked to their horses, mounted, and then headed like they were going out of town.

"Thank You, God. Oh, thank You," she whispered sincerely, with her eyes briefly closed tight.

Now, the only things she had to look out for were her brothers. She had the feeling they wouldn't be far behind, and Tori hoped that she found them before the sheriff did.

eleven

Something was wrong with Victoria Nelson. She wasn't hounding him with a million and one questions, she wasn't snooping through his things, and she wasn't begging him to go outside anymore.

Every day for a week now, she'd come in, smiled politely, smartly discussed the laws she'd studied the night before, thanked him kindly at the end, and left. She was courteous, demure, extremely ladylike, and respectful, not even bringing up the laws she found silly.

Something was definitely wrong with the woman!

Why did he ever think he would want her to be this way—like every other woman in Springton? Where was the spirit that had so frustrated him before? Where was the plainspoken woman that had driven him crazy more times than he could count? Where was the sassy attitude that had once irritated him?

He wanted that woman back!

Sitting in the garden beside his family's house, Billy buried his face in his hands and groaned with confusion. His thoughts made no sense. How could he miss the very things that had tormented him for two months?

"What's wrong with you?"

Billy's head snapped up as Tommy came sauntering along the path to where he sat. "What do you want?" he asked irritably.

Tommy took the bench across from Billy and leaned back in a casual pose with one leg over the other and his arms stretched out along the back. "Since I'm the youngest next to you, I was chosen to find out what's been eating you this last week. Frankly, we're all becoming a little put out by your grumbling and bad attitude." He shook his head. "You've even got Bobby and Danny helping your workers build your house so you can get out of here faster."

Billy threw his brother a wry look, since he knew the statement was a barefaced lie. Every day, Bobby Joe argued with him about staying in the family house. But he understood what Tommy was getting at.

"I've just had something on my mind," he prevaricated, absently grabbing a flower, then methodically ripping the petals off.

"It must be something big to risk mutilating Susannah's flowers like that."

Billy looked down at the crushed yellow rose and sighed. Tossing the flower aside, he stood up and began to pace back and forth. "Aw, Tommy, I just don't know what's going on with me. I have never been so confused in my life."

Tommy was quiet for a moment. "It's got to be a woman if you're that confused, and my guess is it's Tori Nelson."

Billy stopped, throwing a surprised look at Tommy. "Am I that easy to read?"

Tommy shrugged. "Naw, she's just the only female I've seen you around these last few weeks. You're with her every day, so it's easy to figure out she's the one giving you fits."

He sat back down and threw out his arms. "That's just

it! She's not giving me fits! She's acting like a perfect, genteel-born lady."

Tommy arched a brow. "You've lost me."

"It all started when I went and said something stupid. . . ." From there, Billy filled him in on what had happened and how she'd been treating him ever since.

"I still don't get why this bothers you, unless. . ." Tommy's sentence drifted off as an expression of disbelief washed over his face. "Unless you're falling in love with her!"

Just hearing the word was enough to propel Billy off of his seat again and to charge over to Tommy. "Now, hold on a minute! I never said that! I just like her a little, is all."

Tommy stared up at Billy and snorted. "You don't get this upset by just 'liking' a girl."

Irritated, Billy shook his head and stomped back over to his bench. Tommy was wrong. There was no way he was falling in love with Tori. How could he? He had his place in life, and she had hers. A sheriff could not fall in love with someone he'd arrested.

Surely there was a law against it somewhere!

"Well, it doesn't matter, anyhow." Billy looked up to see Tommy's casual expression. "I heard Rance has called on her three times this week. I'm sure we'll be hearing wedding bells 'fore too long."

"Three times!" Billy growled loudly, causing two birds perched in a nearby bush to flutter away. "That's not decent!"

Tommy threw his head back and laughed. "Why ain't it?"

Billy scowled as he scrambled to come up with a reason. He latched onto the one thing he was absolutely sure of.

"He ain't good enough for her!"

"Billy Ray, will you listen to yourself? Weren't you the one who repeatedly said she was a thieving outlaw who needed to be locked in jail?"

"Well. . .maybe I was wrong."

"You mean she didn't steal all those people's valuables?"

Billy sighed. "I mean, she didn't deserve to be locked up in jail." He looked away for a moment, then back to his brother, his eyes solemn. "Tori became a Christian, you know, and it seems as though she really wants to live a different life from the one she lived with her brothers. Still, she's different from most women I know. She has a quick wit, speaks her mind when it's called for, and she seems to care about people. Susannah has told us all how the kids at the orphanage love her."

Billy, realizing his talk was too personal, looked away and hoped his face wasn't turning red.

"Then what's the problem, little brother?" Tommy asked quietly. "What's stopping you from courting her yourself?"

Swallowing, Billy kept his eyes averted. "I'm a sheriff, Tommy. She's my prisoner until the end of this month. It ain't right for me to have any kind of feelings for her."

"Have you prayed about any of this?"

"Of course I've prayed," Billy was quick to answer.

"But have you really prayed about your relationship with Tori?" Tommy lifted his hands up, catching Billy's notice. "What if arresting her on your first day as sheriff was all planned out by God because He knew she was the right person for you?"

Billy thought about that but couldn't believe it. "I just don't think so."

"Is it your career as a sheriff you're worried about? Is it because she's not a woman of our class? Forget all that, Man! If God happens to bring a lady my way who gets into my head and heart the way Tori has yours, little brother, there's nothing in this world that would stop me from making her mine."

The brothers stared at one another for half a minute. Billy knew what Tommy was trying to tell him, but he just couldn't resolve it in his mind. All his life he'd thought about the kind of woman he'd marry, and never did it include a picture of a woman like Tori Nelson.

Why, now, did she seem so appealing?

Thinking about her was wreaking havoc with his mind. He'd always been the type of man who knew exactly where he was going and how he was going to get there. He made plans, he organized, he accomplished.

Since meeting Tori, his organization and plans had flown right out the window.

Tommy finally got up with a long sigh. "So, you gonna at least think about what I've said?"

How could he think about something that didn't make sense to his orderly world? "It's no use, Tommy," he answered softly.

"Then she deserves a man like Rance, who ain't afraid of a woman's past or what other people think about it." He left Billy sitting in the garden, alone.

❧

Three hundred and forty-two. That's how many books were on the shelves in the Aarons' library. They also had twelve crocheted doilies, four Oriental rugs, seven paintings, and six chairs in the room.

Tori knew this for a fact, because for the last half hour, while Rance had been going on and on about how one brands cattle, she'd been improving on her counting skills.

It was just too bad his conversation hadn't improved any!

Rance was a nice man, but Tori couldn't remember ever meeting someone who liked to talk about themselves and what they did for a living as much as he did.

Tori wiggled around in her padded chair and tried to get to a position that would ease the prickly feelings in her feet from sitting in one spot too long. Brushing down the material of her blue polka-dot skirt, she contemplated counting those but decided it would be too much work.

What she longed to do was take a walk outside and smell the fresh air—anything but pretend she was enjoying the attentions of Rance Conway. Her eyes were once again drawn to the huge picture window where she could see the lovely roses blooming radiantly in the Aarons' garden. Tori supposed she could ask Rance to take her for a walk, but she didn't want to encourage him in any way.

Somehow, some way, she was going to have to tell him she wasn't interested in him as a beau.

She sighed and looked back to Rance but nearly choked when she heard what he was saying. "You should see how those varmints wiggle around trying to get away from the branding iron! And when the iron finally makes contact with their hides and you can hear the sizzle of burning—"

"Mr. Conway! We *are* ladies, you know. Some conversations just aren't meant for our delicate ears," Susannah rushed to interrupt as she gave Tori an apologetic glance.

Rance grinned sheepishly. "Aw, Miss Tori, Miss Susannah, I'm sorry about that. I just get plumb carried away when I'm talking about my work."

Susannah smiled at him but then made a show of looking at the watch pinned to her dress. "My goodness, look at the hour. I guess we'll have to say good-bye, Mr. Conway. I'll be needing to get Tori back before sundown."

"Why, I can take Miss Tori home," he offered eagerly while sending Tori a flirtatious smile.

"Oh, I'm afraid I need to talk to Susannah about a few things, Rance, so I'll just have her bring me home," Tori spoke up hurriedly before Susannah could give her consent.

Susannah gave her an odd look, but when Tori answered it with a pleading expression of her own, Susannah nodded. "That's right, I'll just bring her home, but thank you all the same."

Rance's expression fell, but not for long. "Well, can I call on you tomorrow after your lesson with Billy Ray? There's something I'd like to ask you."

Tori felt a lump of dread in her chest at the prospect of what that question could be. She looked at Susannah, who was staring wide-eyed back at her. "Uh, I'm not sure if I can, tomorrow," she hedged.

"Oh, Sugar, I know for a fact you don't have a thing planned!" Susannah exclaimed, wearing an excited smile. When Rance turned back to her, she saw Susannah make a gesture as if she were ringing bells.

Feeling backed into a corner with nowhere to escape, Tori gave Rance a forced smile. "Tomorrow will be fine, then."

Rance's handsome face split into a grin a mile wide. "I'll be waiting for you outside of the sheriff's office." He jumped to his feet and walked over to grab his hat off the hat rack. "Good day, ladies."

"Good day," Tori and Susannah answered in chorus, one less enthusiastic than the other.

As soon as she heard the front door close, Tori whirled around to her friend in a panic. "I can't do this, Susannah! What if he asks me to marry him?"

"That would be wonderful, wouldn't it? Rance would make a fine husband!"

Tori shook her head. "But not for me. I just don't like him that way."

Susannah came over and put her arm around Tori's shoulders. "Now, Sugar, I know he's not the best conversationalist with his talk about burning hide and all, but I'm sure, with time, he'll get better."

"It's not that, Susannah. I can't marry a man I don't love."

Susannah rubbed Tori's back for a moment, then said, "Well, don't make any hasty decisions. Hear him out tomorrow, and then make up your mind." She stood up and looked down at Tori with an understanding smile. "Why don't you take a little stroll through the garden before we leave for Rachel's and pick some of my pretty daisies that you like so well. I couldn't help but notice you looking out the window earlier. It's a great place to do some heavy thinking."

Tori's guilt, she knew, was clearly written on her face. "Was my boredom that noticeable?"

"No. Rance was too caught up in his thrilling story to notice."

They both laughed at that. Susannah waved her toward the French door that led outside and then left the room.

The Aarons' garden was like stepping out into a fairy tale. Flowers of every color of the rainbow were planted in pretty designs along the various walkways. Rich green shrubs set the background for each arrangement, and in the center a breathtaking fountain showered water onto a round pond made of stone.

It was unlike anything Tori had ever seen. She didn't see much greenery out in the desert-covered West where she'd spent the last few years of her life, except maybe cactus.

Closing her eyes, she deeply breathed in all the glorious aromas that surrounded her. She could only identify one kind of flower smell—the yellow roses that were the main plant of the garden. But to her, the roses paled in comparison to the daisies. She loved them because they'd been her mother's favorite flower and she'd always worn them in her hair.

It was sad how she could remember a flower but not what her mother had looked like.

The clearest memory she had of her parents was of one Christmas when they'd been sitting around a little tree strung with popcorn and homemade decorations. Pa, as she remembered, had a beautiful, deep voice, and he'd led them in singing carols while strumming his guitar. Ma had been holding Tori in her arms, rocking gently back and forth, humming along while brushing her hand down her daughter's long hair. Kyle and Scott were having a difficult time between singing and licking the candy canes Pa had given each of them.

They had been a happy family, her brothers had assured her of that, since they had more memories than she had.

One day, maybe they could be one again. . . .

Slowly, she walked down one of the paths, taking her time to capture every detail of her surroundings. When she got back to Rachel's house, she would write down everything so she would never forget it. She wanted to remember too, to thank God for allowing her to experience so many of His beautiful creations all at one time.

Then, to her surprise, a group of butterflies suddenly fluttered across her path as if they were doing a dance around her head. Laughing, Tori spread out her arms and twirled around, taking giddy pleasure in just being young and free.

She'd so seldom felt like that in her short life. She wanted to hang onto it, to savor it, just in case she never felt that way again.

If only her brothers could feel this way. If only they could be handed an opportunity like she'd been so blessed with.

If only. . .

"Hello, Tori." A man's voice brought her back down to earth in a hurry.

She stopped spinning, pushed her fallen curls from her face, and looked into the bright blue eyes of Billy Ray Aaron.

twelve

When Billy had rounded the curve of the path and come across Tori frolicking about with the butterflies, he'd been swept away by the sheer beauty of her unguarded expression and the joy of her laughter.

For a moment, Billy let himself contemplate the words Tommy had offered him. What if God had brought her into his life to be his wife? What if he let himself believe it was all right to court her, all right to fall in love with her?

It was so tempting to believe it—so easy to give in to his attraction for her.

So simple to make the dream come true.

He folded his arms across his chest and his hand brushed against the cold metal star pinned to his vest. Reality crashed around his head, and the dream dissipated as quickly as it had come.

"Hello, Tori," he said, just to stop the enchantment of the scene before him.

She stopped and stared at him with her beautiful hair falling about her face and shoulders. "Sheriff," she murmured.

Billy forced himself to look away. "I didn't know you were here." He winced at the idiocy of how his words sounded.

"Susannah invited Rance to call on me here," she explained, her hands trying vainly to put some order to her flyaway locks.

Jealousy sprang up like an ugly monster at hearing Rance's name, but he quickly squelched it. He had no right to care that she was being courted. He had no right to feel as though he was letting something important pass him up by not courting her himself.

It wasn't his business. He had made the choice, and he must live with it.

Instead, he focused on the trouble she seemed to be having with her hair. "Let me help you," he offered as he came closer to her and, taking her by the shoulders, turned her back to him.

He smiled at the wary look she gave him as she handed him a ribbon, but he motioned for her to face forward, then proceeded to gather her thick hair at the nape of her neck.

"Are you sure you know what you're doing?"

He grinned again, enjoying the silky feeling of her hair running through his fingers. "My niece was without a mother for a couple of years before Bobby Joe remarried —her mother died when Beth was four. We all had to tie her ribbons at one time or another."

He managed a pretty good bow, then playfully tugged on her hair before turning her back around. "All done!" he exclaimed.

But when he started to remove his hands from her shoulders, he made the terrible mistake of looking into her pretty blue eyes. She was smiling up at him, and there was something in her face, shining in her gaze. It seemed to mirror the emotions he'd just felt a moment ago when he watched her with those butterflies.

The emotions that had returned suddenly came in full force.

He wanted to kiss her, and the more he thought on it, the better it sounded.

So, he did.

So very gently their lips met in the sweetest kiss Billy had ever experienced. It was like Christmas, birthdays, and the Fourth of July all wrapped up in one tiny moment of time. Although he'd only kissed two other girls in his lifetime, neither of them made him feel like Tori did—like the luckiest man alive.

He started to wrap his arms around her, when she unexpectedly broke the kiss and backed away from him. Before he could gather his wits or even open his eyes, a resounding slap was laid, none too gently, across his cheek.

His eyes were open now and were glaring at Tori, trying to comprehend what had just happened. "What was that for?"

Tori, cheeks flushed and breathless, cast an accusing glare back at him. "You kissed me!" she blurted out.

Billy threw his arms in the air. "Yeah, so?"

"It's improper for a man to kiss a woman he's not courting. Susannah said so!"

"Is it proper for a woman who is not being courted by the man who kissed her to kiss him back?" Billy flung back.

Tori's eyes narrowed, and with her hands on her hips and toe tapping, she returned, "I was taken off guard. You took advantage of my inexperience!"

"Lady, if you flash those eyes at a man the way you were doing earlier with me, then you can expect to be kissed!"

She gasped. "I was not—*flashing*—my eyes at you! And besides, you warned me about even touching your arm the other day! Where did that rule go?"

"First, you answer my question! What's been wrong with you this last week?"

"What do you mean?"

"You've been acting funny, not like yourself," he emphasized, jabbing a finger at her.

Tori put a hand to her chest. "I've been acting like a perfect lady!"

"Well, I don't like it! I want you to go back to acting like you used to!"

Billy knew he wasn't making any sense by the way Tori was looking at him. "I don't get it! You fuss at me whether I act one way or another. Why don't you just admit to yourself you plain don't like me?"

"I can't because I do like you! There, are you happy?" he yelled back without thinking.

Appalled at what had just come out of his mouth, he tried to think of a way to undo it.

Tori blinked a couple of times in astonishment. "You *like* me?"

Billy swallowed and decided there was nothing else to do but be straight with her. "Yeah, but don't get any ideas about it. My attraction to you is completely against my better judgment."

An expression of hurt swept over her lovely features, but it didn't stay long. Anger swiftly took its place.

"Why, you conceited, arrogant. . ." She sputtered as if trying to come up with the right words to express the way she felt. "First, you kiss me, and then you tell me not to get any ideas! You're taking it for granted that I even care if you like me or not! Well—I don't!"

She didn't like him? Her words were like a blow to his gut, but he wasn't about to show it.

"Well—good!" he blustered. "Then we can just forget this whole thing ever happened."

Her chin rose a notch as she crossed her arms at her chest. "Fine and dandy with me."

It was a battle of wills as they stared at one another, putting on faces of indifference and maybe challenging each other a little as to who would look away first.

The contest was taken out of their hands when Susannah called out for Tori.

"I guess I'll be going, Sheriff Aaron," Tori told him haughtily. But before she could escape, he stopped her.

"Would you just call me Billy. Calling me Sheriff is a little ridiculous after that kiss, don't you think?"

"What kiss would that be?" she sniffed.

He let out a heavy breath, wishing he'd never lashed out at her with those stupid words. "Look, Tori, I'm sorry. I shouldn't have lost my temper and said those mean things."

She thought about that for a minute. "What part, exactly, are you sorry for saying?" she asked casually.

He grinned. "Everything after the part where I said I liked you."

She looked down, a blush rising on her cheeks. "Well, I didn't mean it when I said I didn't like you, either."

"What about the conceited, arrogant part?"

"Well, I guess I'll apologize for that too, although I truly believed it when I said it."

"That's your idea of an apology?"

She gave him an innocent look. "I'm just telling the truth."

Billy chuckled and held out his hand. "Why don't we just agree to at least try to be friends. Think we can manage that for two and a half more weeks?"

Tori took his hand and grinned gingerly. "Do friends kiss each other like we did today?"

He gave her a teasing look and winked. "What kiss?"

Shaking her head at him, she laughed and ran back to the house.

What kiss? When he was ninety-two and two steps away from the grave, he would still remember kissing Tori Nelson on a summer's day in the middle of a rose garden with the butterflies flying about them. It would be a memory that would hopefully brighten a day when he felt down or lonely.

Today, however, knowing that he would never again get to kiss her did nothing but depress him.

Then it occurred to him, except for mentioning that Rance had come by to visit her, she hadn't mentioned him again. There'd been no accusation flung back that he shouldn't kiss her because Rance was courting her. No warning him away or that her beau wouldn't tolerate such behavior.

Instead she'd slapped him because Susannah told her she ought to.

He knew he shouldn't be excited about that morsel of information—but he was.

❧

Tori could tell the moment Susannah saw her coming through the French doors of the library that her friend suspected something was up.

"Goodness, me! I declare, you are positively glowing.

That walk in the garden did all that?" her friend asked in a casual tone, although suspicion was clearly in her eyes.

Tori was bursting to tell someone about what she'd experienced with Billy. That kiss was better than anything she'd ever imagined it could be. And it also sealed in her heart the fact she had to end things with Rance.

Susannah walked up to Tori curiously and put a hand on her cheek. "Well? You going to tell me or not?"

"Billy Ray just kissed me out in the garden!" she blurted out, not knowing any other way to say it.

Susannah's mouth gaped as she stared in stunned astonishment at Tori. "He didn't!" she finally said, clearly scandalized at the thought. "Bobby's going to have to knock some sense into that boy. It's just not like him to take advantage of a lady like that!"

Tori shook her head. "I'm afraid I already did that. The moment I gathered my wits about me, I slapped him across the face, just like you told me I should."

Susannah laughed with glee. "I surely wish I could've seen that! I'm sure he deserved it!"

"Oh, Susannah, it wasn't like that. I—well—I wanted him to kiss me," she said, embarrassed at her brazen admission.

"You did?" Susannah's expression changed as she studied her friend more closely. "As I live and breathe! That's why you aren't interested in Rance. You're in love with Billy Ray."

Having Susannah put it into simple, straightforward words like that suddenly made everything clear. "I guess I am." Her voice was filled with the wonder of discovery.

Susannah spun around, clasping her hands under her

chin. "There it was, staring me in the face all this time and I didn't even see it. I knew he was acting jealous over Rance stepping out with you, but I never dreamed he'd relax his strict code of duty and start pursuing you!"

Tori's smile faded as she was confronted with the reality of the situation. "He's not pursuing me. He said liking me is completely against his will."

She gasped. "Why, that scamp! That's terrible!"

"Oh, he apologized for saying it, but I know he meant it." Her eyes suddenly filled with tears, and she threw herself into Susannah's arms. "I'm so confused!" she wailed. "Why did I have to go and kiss him? He's a lawman, for goodness' sake! Why couldn't I have the good sense to fall for Rance? At least he wants to marry meeeee. . . ."

Susannah patted her back in a motherly fashion. "There, there, Sugar. I'm sure it's not as bad as all that. Billy just doesn't know what's good for him is all. He just needs a little help."

That piqued Tori's interest. Pushing back to look at her friend, she swiped her eyes with her sleeves, ignoring the wince Susannah made at the unladylike gesture. "What do ya—mean—help?" she asked between tearful hiccups.

Susannah smiled serenely. "Did you know Bobby Joe first asked me to marry him solely for the purpose of being a mother for his daughter? He wanted a marriage in name only! Can you fathom that?" Susannah shook her head, causing the red ringlets at her temples to bounce about. "So, I set out to make him realize that he loved me and that he wanted me for a real wife. Of course, it took a nightmare of a trip all the way to Charleston to do the trick, but he finally came around to my way of thinking!"

Tori was amazed. Susannah and Bobby Joe always seemed so in love with one another.

Thinking about what her friend had said, she asked, "I'm not going to have to drag him to the Carolinas just to get him to fall in love with me, am I?"

Susannah laughed. "No, Sugar! You've got something even better—Billy's undivided attention for a half hour of every weekday." She winked at Tori. "Use it to your advantage!"

More confused than anything, Tori tried to imagine herself flirting with the sheriff, but it was just too crazy to contemplate. "I'm not sure how to go about it."

Putting her arm around Tori, Susannah led her out of the library. "You just be yourself, because that's what he's attracted to. Billy's got the idea that because he arrested you, it's just not acceptable for him to fall in love with you and court you." She shook her head. "That boy has more self-inflicted rules than anybody I've ever seen. But we've got to make him see beyond his rules. We've got to make him open up his eyes and heart and see what God has practically dropped in his lap."

Tori was still doubtful. "I think he'd like to forget the day I 'dropped in.' "

Susannah was undaunted. "You just never mind that. Leave everything to me!"

thirteen

As Tori walked toward the sheriff's office the next day, her mind was clouded not only with worry over seeing Billy again, but she was still on the lookout for Doogan McConnell. So far, she hadn't seen him again, but Tori wasn't going to quit watching for him.

Nearing the door of the office, she slowed her steps a bit, a little scared and a little embarrassed to face him. How would he act toward her? Would he be back to his normal grouchy self, or would he act more friendly?

Honestly, Tori wasn't sure how she wanted him to treat her. If he was bad-tempered, it would sure go a long way to keep things from being awkward. On the other hand, when he looked at her with a smile in his eyes, it made her feel as though she were floating on a cloud of happiness.

Things were a lot simpler before Sheriff Billy Ray Aaron barged into her life!

Realizing she didn't want him to catch her just standing at his door again, Tori grabbed the large brass handle and let herself in. After a quick glance around the small, uncluttered room, she realized all her anxiety would have to be endured a little longer. Sheriff Billy wasn't there.

Tori heard a shuffling sound come from the cells and whirled around expecting to see Billy. Instead, she was shocked to find a man staring at her with narrow dark eyes who was definitely not the sheriff! He was a thin man dressed in dusty black pants and shirt with a red bandanna tied around his neck. He was lying with his head propped up on one of the sturdy wooden cots in cell number two. A sinister smile creased his whiskered face, and those eerie dark eyes boldly perused her person in an ungentlemanly manner. Everything about the prisoner made her skin crawl with revulsion. He was a man who lived his life without morals or religious convictions. His face held only cold emptiness.

A face she'd instantly recognized.

She had not seen the man called "Vega" since the day she'd run into McConnell. The only time they'd come face-to-face was in Amarillo, when he'd almost caught her after her brothers had been arrested.

Did he recognize her? Usually she could read a person's eyes or expression, but this man's face held nothing but pure evil.

Then she saw it, that slight change in his eyes. He carefully hid it, but it was too late. She knew he'd recognized her, but from the way he studied her, she could tell he hadn't figured out why, yet.

Well, she wasn't going to give him a chance. As if fire were breathing down her neck, Tori flew toward the door and into the arms of the sheriff.

"Whoa there, Tori. You alright?" he asked as he pulled her back away from him and studied her with concern.

Tori looked around him and saw the door was wide open. She'd been so stunned to recognize the prisoner, she hadn't even heard him come in. Biting her lip, she sought Billy's eyes. "I'm okay. He just startled me is all."

Billy seemed surprised. "I wouldn't figure somebody

like him would spook you. Didn't you sort of run with—"

"Would you be quiet!" she hissed at him, trying to be as quiet as she could. "I know who he is!"

It took only a moment for the seriousness of her words and expression to wipe the teasing smile from his lips. He studied her pleading eyes while conveying to Tori he would take care of everything.

Billy's handsome face hardened as he looked back up to where the prisoner lay. "Why don't we take a little walk by the creek and get some fresh air," he said loud enough to be heard by the prisoner, then took her elbow and led her from the office.

They were almost to the creek when Billy turned her toward him, bringing them both to a stop. "Okay, Nelson. Spill it. Who is Eugene Vega to you?"

"Vega is one of Doogan McConnell's men. McConnell had my brothers arrested. They've been trying to track me for two years now."

Those calmly spoken words might as well have been dynamite to Billy, because he blew up at hearing them. "You are being tracked down by thugs like Vega, and you didn't think to tell me this? Nelson, do you think you're invincible? Don't you think that maybe, just maybe, they could have grabbed you before I would know what's happening?"

Oh, boy, was he mad. But it didn't matter so much under the circumstances. Actually, it felt kind of nice that he was so concerned about her well-being.

"I'm sorry, Billy, but I haven't seen them in over a year. What did you arrest him for?"

Billy shook his head. "He got drunk last night and started

shooting out the windows of the saloon. He had the money to pay for the damage, but I was going to hold him a few days just to make sure he knows we don't tolerate such behavior here."

Tori groaned. "If he's back in town, that means McConnell isn't far behind. What if they found out about me? They think I have that stupid diamond."

The sheriff shook his head as if trying to clear it. "Wait a minute. What diamond?"

Maybe it was because she'd had to carry the burden alone for two years that she poured out the whole sad story to him. Maybe it was because he really seemed concerned for her.

Maybe she was beginning not only to love him but also to trust him.

After she finished, Billy thought for a minute as he absently ran a calloused hand down his tanned cheek. "And you don't know who has the diamond?"

Tori shook her head. "I don't have a clue. All I know is I don't have it and neither did my brothers."

Billy propped his hands on his hips and gazed off to the horizon, the morning sun glinting in his blue eyes. He made such a handsome picture standing there, concerned over her situation. She knew he cared about her. She only wished he would let himself love her.

But wishes were not going to make her situation any better. She was going to have to come clean on everything in order for the sheriff to be able to help her. He needed to know she trusted him. She needed to gain his trust too.

"There's something else you need to know. Uh, something I should have told you."

Billy brought his attention back to her wary expression. "Is this going to make things worse?"

"Probably."

He sighed. "Alright, tell me everything. I want the whole story."

"Well, I happened to see Doogan McConnell just about a week or so ago, here, in Springton."

His jaw was clenching and unclenching so fast Tori thought for sure he was going to crack a tooth. "And did McConnell happen to see you?" he managed to ask.

Tori swallowed with nervousness, unsure of how Billy was going to take her answer. She soon found out. "Uh, not only did he see me, we exchanged a few words."

"I don't believe this!" he growled, lifting his arms up and walking away from her. He soon turned back and stomped up to her, taking her by the arms. "What did he say to you? Did he recognize you? Threaten you in any way?"

"If you would stop shaking me, I'll tell you!"

Chagrined, Billy immediately loosened his grip, but he kept his hands where they were.

She continued. "He didn't recognize me, but he was asking a lot of questions. He's looking for a boy, but he could easily find out the details of my arrest and how I was dressed." She shook her head. "Billy, if he finds me, he'll have me arrested for stealing the diamond whether I have it or not. He's got witnesses that connect me with my brothers. Just the fact that I ran away makes me look guilty!"

"They'll have to go through me first!" he declared with vehemence as he pulled her into his arms. "Don't worry, Tori. I'm not going to let them accuse you of something you're innocent of."

Tori may have been surprised at his emotional reaction, but goodness knew, she wasn't going to question it! Closing her eyes, she leaned into his solid chest and wrapped her arms around his waist.

"I'm not completely innocent, Billy," she murmured. "I was a thief, and I have stolen things before. Maybe I do belong in jail."

His grip tightened. "Tori, you did the things you did because you didn't know better. But you do now. And not only that, you've become a Christian. That means you're a new person inside."

For a moment more, Tori enjoyed the feel of his strong arms and the steady beat of his heart. But his embrace was only a reaction and therefore temporary. If she stayed in his arms, she would only feel worse because it wasn't a forever kind of hug.

Stepping back from him, she braced her hands on his chest to put space between them. "I know I'm different, Billy. And I know God has granted me mercy and grace in this situation here in Springton. If I have to spend the rest of my life in jail, all this would have been worth it. I've got friends, and I have Jesus in my heart. I would still be a blessed person."

Billy shook his head. "Don't give up, Tori. Even if McConnell decides to come back, he's going to have a fight on his hands."

Tori smiled at his fervent expression. "For someone who wanted me in jail in the first place and one who likes me against his will, you sure are willing to go to great lengths to help me."

Billy's eyes narrowed at her teasing tone as he folded

his arms. "I thought I'd already apologized for saying both of those things."

She put up her hands in surrender. "You're right. I shouldn't have brought it up."

He nodded, though he looked disturbed that the subject had been brought up. "Well, I guess we better get on back to the jail. I'll grab my law books, and we can go up to my house to do the lessons today. I'm sure Susannah will be there."

He reached out to take hold of her and escort her back to town, but Tori grabbed his arm first. "Wait, there's just one more thing."

"Don't tell me there's somebody else after you!"

She winced at his exasperated expression. "Well, sort of. You see, my brothers have escaped from prison, and I believe they're on their way to protect me from McConnell," she quickly blurted out in one breath.

Billy frowned. "And how is it you know about them escaping?"

"I saw a telegram on your desk a few weeks back alerting you about their escape."

Suspicion marred his face as he stared at her. "So, you stole it," he deduced, his tone scathing.

"Yes, but only because I was scared you'd jump at the chance to arrest them." She took his hand and looked at him imploringly. "You've got to understand, Billy. If my brothers have escaped, it's because they know I'm in danger. They only had a few more years to go on their sentences. I just didn't want them hurt."

Billy shook his head and pulled her hand to his chest. "And you thought I'd hurt them?"

"I thought you'd use them to get back at me."

He let out a long breath. "I'm sorry you had that impression of me. But you've got to know, now, that I'm not that type of a person. I *will* have to bring them in, yes, but I will listen to what they have to say too."

Sheriff Billy Aaron was a really good man. She'd seen a whole different side of him in recent weeks. A side she loved more and more each day.

Could Susannah be right? Could there be a way for the sheriff to fall in love with her too? He liked her, she knew. Could he feel more and just not realize it?

Night after night she prayed God would guide her path. And day after day, she found Sheriff Billy right in the middle of that path. Of course, there was also Rance.

But she didn't love Rance. She didn't want to be his wife.

Pushing her confusing thoughts aside, she smiled at him. "I know you'll be fair."

She pulled at his hand to walk back to town, but he tugged her back. "Are you sure that's all you need to tell me? No more deep, dark secrets that I should be concerned about?"

"No, that's it," she told him, but in her heart she knew it was a lie. She did have one more secret, but it was one he'd never find out about, unless by some miracle he realized he loved her back.

"Good!" he said with great relief. "Let's go get those books."

He held tight to her hand as he pulled her toward the sheriff's office.

Tori didn't question the reasons Billy kept a hold on her hand; she just enjoyed how it made her feel. For a brief moment in time, she could pretend they were courting—that they'd been out for a walk, just to be alone with each other.

But those wishful thoughts scattered like leaves in the wind the moment they began to cross the street to where the sheriff's office was.

Rance was waiting there in his wagon. And it was clear from the thunder brewing on his face that he'd noticed they were holding hands.

fourteen

Billy didn't know if it was the possessive way Rance was glaring at Tori or just plain old jealousy on his part, but for some reason he deliberately held fast to Tori's hand. He looked at her to see what her reaction was, and when he saw the dread on her face as she stared at the cowboy, he felt like crowing like a rooster.

This was not the look of a woman in love. A woman in love would have dropped his hand like a hot potato and run to greet her beau.

Then again, a woman in love would not have held his hand in the first place. She wouldn't have let him hold her as he had by the creek.

She certainly wouldn't have let him kiss her as she had in his garden.

Suddenly, everything became so clear to him. Every look, every touch, every word that had passed between them should have been obvious to him, and would have been, had his own emotions not clouded his mind.

Victoria Nelson, his reformed thief, wasn't in love with Rance Conway. She was in love—with him.

Before he could let that incredible thought sink in, Tori had slipped her hand from his and was making her way to where Rance was. He followed slowly, and when he reached them, he picked up on what Rance was saying to her.

"I packed us a lunch and thought we'd have our talk down by the creek." He shifted his eyes to Billy and frowned. "But it looks like you've already been that direction."

"Got a prisoner in the jail today, Rance. Didn't think it would be a fittin' place to do our lesson," Billy explained, not wanting to cause a rift between himself and his friend.

Rance seemed to accept this excuse, although Billy could tell he wasn't totally accepting of their being out alone together. "Well, are you ready to go?" He directed his question to Tori.

She hesitated a moment, then nodded her head. Billy felt like his heart was being ripped out of his chest as she let Rance help her into the wagon and sat beside him. He wanted so badly to jump up on the rig and haul her back down with him. He could tell her he knew how she felt. He could let her know he'd been feeling the same way.

But he felt frozen, unable to grasp exactly what all these new revelations meant to him. What they meant to both of them.

He might have talked himself out of doing anything at all, had she not looked back at him just as they had turned the corner to the road that led to the creek. The lovely blue eyes that met his own were wistful, the curve of her small mouth, sad.

She didn't want to go. And he surely did not want her to go.

Then why in the world wasn't he doing something about it?

Spurred into action, he started running to where the wagon was heading. He might have caught up with them had it not been for his brothers stepping into his path at that very moment.

"Whoa, there, little brother! Where are you heading to in such a hurry?" Danny asked, catching him by the arm when Billy attempted to go around them.

He yanked against Danny's hold. "I ain't got time for this, Dan. I've got to catch that wagon!"

Just as he broke free, his other arm was captured by Tommy. "Oh, no. You're not going to run after Rance and Tori and mess up Rance's big proposal."

"His *what?*" Billy asked, shocked to his core.

"Rance is going to ask Tori to marry him. Susannah told us so herself," Danny supplied.

"Not if I can help it!" Billy yelled and tried once again to break free.

"Just how do you plan to stop him from proposing? You planning on making a proposal of your own?"

Billy ignored the question, commenting instead, "She's in love with me, not Rance."

Tommy shrugged. "Maybe so, but Rance is the only one I see willing to marry her and not just play around with her feelings by stealing kisses when you think no one's looking!"

Billy's face burned with embarrassment. "How did you know?"

"You forget both our rooms look out over the garden."

Danny nodded. "You gave us quite a show, little brother."

"And since you'd just told me you couldn't marry a girl like Tori, I didn't think it quite proper for you to be kissing her!"

Tommy and Billy stared at one another for a moment, and

Billy could feel his brothers' disapproval of him. It made him feel ashamed of how he'd felt toward Tori—how he'd believed that she somehow wasn't good enough for him.

But it didn't matter what her background was or what she'd done in the past. How could he let himself throw away a chance at happiness with such a wonderful woman simply because she hadn't had the privilege of being brought up in a stable, wealthy family as he had?

He looked at both of his brothers and stated firmly, "Rance isn't the only one willing to offer marriage. I aim to make an offer of my own!"

Billy watched with suspicion as Tommy and Danny looked at each other with a knowing grin, then back to him. "Susannah told us that with a little nudging you'd come to see the light."

"What is that supposed to mean?"

Danny shook his head. "Who do you think sent us over here?"

Billy scowled. "This isn't none of her business—or yours for that matter!"

Tommy shook his head wisely. "Susannah makes everything concerning the family her business, and we wouldn't dare say nay against her!"

"Well, tell her she succeeded!" he said with exasperation. "Now, if you'd kindly step out of the way, I will try to catch up with them."

His brothers parted and let Billy slip between them. "Now don't go and make an enemy of Rance. He's liable to get his heart broken over this!" Danny called out.

"You might want to tell him Lola Mae Bramlett is rumored to have a crush on him. Knowing Rance, he won't be so brokenhearted he wouldn't want to take advantage of a situation if it presented itself."

Billy smiled at Tommy's comment as he ran toward the creek and hoped his brother was right. He didn't want to hurt his friend, but he also didn't want Tori to feel pressured into a loveless marriage, especially since he was willing to offer one that would be filled with more love and happiness than either of them had ever dreamed.

As he drew near the creek, he was surprised to see Rance riding past him, alone. He looked upset and didn't even glance in Billy's direction as he urged his horses to go faster.

Quickly, he scanned the bank of the creek until he saw her.

There she stood, her back to him, silhouetted against the great trunks of the tall pines that bordered the creek. Streams of light shone through the trees, casting a golden glow against her hair and calico print dress.

The twigs cracking beneath his feet alerted Tori to his presence, but a slight movement of her head was the only indication she gave that she was aware of him. She reached up and appeared to swipe at her face with her sleeve, and he could hear a small sniffle. Why was she crying? Obviously she didn't give Rance the answer he wanted to hear. So, why was *she* crying?

He stepped close to her and reached out to put a comforting arm around her when she spoke. "If that's you, Billy Ray Aaron, you can just turn yourself around and march on back to your precious sheriff's office."

So startled at her scornful words, he could only sputter, "Excuse me?"

Whirling around, she glared at him through red, tear-stained eyes. "This is all *your* fault, you know!" she said, poking him in the chest for emphasis. "I could be celebrating my engagement to a very nice man instead of crying over how much I just hurt him by saying no!" She shook her head in frustration. "Why in the world did you have to start being nice to me? Why did you kiss me and act so jealous over my seeing Rance? Why did you have to act so caring and protective of me?"

"Because I lo—"

"Just be quiet and let me finish!" she ordered, poking his chest again. "I've lived my whole life dreaming of having a real family, living with a man who'd love me and who'd give my children the kind of life I didn't get to have. And five minutes ago, I had that dream presented to me, all wrapped up pretty with a bow on top. And what did I do?"

She closed her eyes and groaned, turning away from him and facing the creek once again. "I turned it down, is what I did. All because I had the misfortune to fall in love with you instead of Rance."

She looked toward the sky. "You, who likes me, but not enough to risk your reputation or your precious pride by courting me."

Hearing her say she loved him filled him with so much happiness, he thought his heart would burst with it. Taking her by the shoulders, he turned her toward him. "Listen, Tori, I don't just like you; I'm in love with you too. I should have realized it before this, but I was just too wrapped up in myself and my job to notice. Please give me a chance to make up for my stupidity."

She looked up at him, seemingly dazed by his declaration.

He framed her face with his hands, smoothing back her silky hair, caressing her soft skin. "Sweetheart, I believe with all my heart that God meant for us to find one another. He must have known just what kind of loving, caring woman I needed and what kind of ornery, temperamental lawman you needed." She laughed softly up at him. "And He found a way to bring you to Springton," he finished on a more serious note.

"I've been a Christian for most of my life, but you sure couldn't tell it by my recent actions. I've been prideful, arrogant, and judgmental. I've asked God to forgive me. Now I'm asking for you to."

Tori covered one of his hands with her own and snuggled her cheek into his rough palm. "I forgive you, Billy, and you need to forgive me too. I may be a new Christian, but I'm learning I need to listen to Him before I spout off words that I shouldn't say. I was prejudiced against you and your position."

Billy smiled and folded her into his embrace. "There is nothing to forgive, Darlin'. I'm just glad you turned poor ole Rance down. It would have been a lot worse if I had to burst into the middle of your wedding ceremony and carry you off before you could say the 'I do's."

Tori pulled back to look at him. "You wouldn't have!"

He smiled cockily. "Oh yes, I would have. You belong to me, not that smooth-talking cowboy."

"Now, you be nice to Rance. I really hurt his feelings by turning him down," she scolded.

"I know," he replied soberly. "I hate that it was my fault he got as far as a proposal."

Billy let go of her shoulders and linked his hands with Tori's, drawing them close to his heart. "Now, I know you've already been asked this once today, but I just can't wait another minute to ask it for myself." He bent and placed a gentle kiss on her hands. "Victoria Nelson, I'm a man with faults, as you have found out in recent weeks, and I may not have been what you had in mind when you dreamed of a husband, but I promise to love and protect you for the rest of my life if you'll just let me. Will you do me the honor of becoming my wife?"

Billy watched with awe as tears filled her beautiful eyes and a smile as radiant as the morning sun curved her lips. "You are exactly what I've dreamed of, Billy. Except, of course, for the part about you being a lawman," she admitted with her usual candor, making them both chuckle. "But before I say yes, you have to understand that McConnell still could have me arrested for stealing the diamond. Billy, I'd hate for us to start out our lives with that fear hanging over our heads."

Just hearing the name McConnell sent waves of anger through his body. To know there was someone out there who wanted to do Tori harm, to accuse her of something she was innocent of, made him want to hunt the man down before he could get to Tori. "You listen to me, Darlin'. My family has a lot of connections in this state, and I'll do whatever I can to clear you of any charges McConnell wants to throw at you."

"That won't be necessary, Lawman," a man's voice abruptly intruded on their conversation.

Standing there, across the creek, on the other side of the small bridge, stood a tall, blond man. He was dressed in dusty, worn blue pants that had seen better days and an ill-fitted chambray shirt with the sleeves cut off inches below the shoulder.

However, all Billy saw now was the pistol the man was aiming right at his chest.

"Kyle!" Tori suddenly cried, and before Billy knew it, she'd let go of his hands and was running across the narrow bridge.

"Tori, don't!" he yelled, for all the good it did. She'd already launched herself into the man's arms, squeezing him around the neck.

Still, that gun never moved from its target.

Billy dearly hoped the man was one of her brothers, or else he was going to be quite upset.

He started to go after her when he heard the sound of the gun being cocked, freezing him where he stood. That the man could even think with Tori crying, talking, and kissing him on the cheeks was amazing to Billy.

"Tori, can you please tell him to put his gun down, that shooting a sheriff has a guaranteed sentence of hanging!" he yelled, hoping Tori would have the wits about her to hear him.

Thankfully, she did. Jumping back from the man, she gasped when she saw the gun, then promptly yanked it out of his hand and uncocked it all in one movement.

The woman was truly amazing.

"Aw, I wasn't going to shoot him. I ain't that crazy. I just wanted to scare him a little," the tough man replied, taking the gun from her and putting it back in his holster.

Tori shook her head and smiled back at Billy. "This is my brother, Kyle. Kyle, this is the man I'm going to marry, Sheriff Billy Aaron."

Kyle scowled at his sister. "I knew you'd go and do something stupid without me and Scott looking after ya. Well, the good news is, you ain't married yet." He took her by the arm and started pulling her toward the woods. "In a week or so, you'll forget 'im!"

In two seconds flat, Billy was over the bridge with his own pistol cocked and aimed at Kyle Nelson. "You'll take her over my dead body, Nelson," he growled, his arm steady and sure.

Faster than anyone Billy had ever seen, Kyle turned in a flash and had his own pistol directed toward the sheriff once again. "That, Lawman, can be arranged."

fifteen

Tori looked from her brother to Billy and had to marvel at the way grown men could suddenly act like five year olds fighting over a toy. Her brother, with all his rough ways, had never shot a man in his whole life. And Billy wasn't about to shoot the brother of the woman he'd just proposed marriage to.

But there they were, aiming their pistols at each other like two gunfighters with a score to settle.

With a long-suffering sigh, she folded her arms across her chest and marched right in between them. "Billy, put the gun down. Kyle is not going to drag me off anywhere." She turned to her brother. "And you! Stop acting like you're used to pointing a gun at somebody and tell me where Scott is!"

It took a few seconds before the men, at the same time, of course, holstered their guns. There was still an air of readiness radiating from them, though—one just waiting for the other to make a move.

Tori gave Kyle a nudge, trying to bring his attention to her. "Are you going to tell me where Scott is? Is he hurt?"

Kyle's gaze remained on the sheriff, but he answered. "Scott is in Waco. We found out what happened to the diamond and what McConnell's plans for you are. We broke out and once we got to Waco, we found out McConnell's brother, Lachlan, is the one who took the jewel. Scott is going to get a signed statement, saying that Lachlan, not we, stole the diamond."

"How is he going to manage to do that?" Billy asked suspiciously.

Kyle smiled grimly. "By any means he can. There's no way we're going to let McConnell have Tori arrested. She's managed, so far, to keep from being arrested. I'm not going to let her go to jail for something she didn't do."

Tori bit her lower lip as she looked up at her overprotective brother. "Uh, I'm afraid I no longer have a clean record. I was arrested for picking pockets two and a half months ago."

Kyle grew considerably upset at that news. "And just who arrested you? Him?" he asked scathingly, pointing an accusing finger in Billy's direction.

"Well, yes, but—"

"She didn't go to jail," Billy interjected. "No one would press charges, so the judge gave her a sort of probation. She was sent to live with Reverend Stone and his wife."

Kyle turned to Tori and really looked at her for the first time. "Is that why you're dressed like a girl?" he criticized.

She bristled at that. "I *am* a girl, Kyle." She took a deep breath and continued. "I'm different now. I've not only changed the way I dress and act, but I've become a Christian too."

Kyle didn't seem to know what to say to that, and Tori knew he didn't fully understand what she was telling him.

He shook his head and went back to their original topic of conversation. "So, if he is the one who arrested you, why in the world are you marrying him?"

"Because I love him, Kyle," she stated simply, pleading

with her eyes for her brother to understand.

"If you had to fall in love with someone, couldn't you have picked someone that wasn't connected to the law?"

"I picked him, Kyle, because he has a good heart, just like you and Scott," she answered, laying her hand gently on his rough, weathered cheek.

Then he did something he hadn't done since she was a little girl—he hugged her to him and planted a kiss on top of her head. "Aw, I've missed you, Tori. Did you know you look just like our mama did? I could've sworn it was her standing across the creek when I spotted you there."

Tears sprang to her eyes as she hugged him back. It was so good to be able to see him again, to be able to speak to him. Tori had missed them both so much.

"Tori," Billy called sensitively. "You know I'm going to have to take him in. He's an escaped prisoner. I don't have a choice."

Tori held onto Kyle tighter. "No, please, Billy. Why can't you just let him go?"

It was Kyle who answered her. "It's alright, Tori." He pulled her back away from him so she could look him in the eye. "We always knew we'd have to go back to jail. After we cleared your name and made sure you were safe, we planned on turning ourselves in."

Tori knew Kyle was doing the right thing, but it still hurt to know her brothers were going to have to spend more time behind bars. She went over to Billy and held onto his arm. "Billy, isn't there anything you can do?" she pleaded, all the while knowing she was interfering with his job.

Billy covered her hand and looked over at Kyle. "If your

brother can get that statement, I'll see what I can do about getting you both reduced sentences. In the meantime, I'll let it be known you came to me and turned yourself in. It'll look better when your case is brought up."

Tori squeezed his arm in thanks and she saw Kyle nodding his head.

Everything has to work out, she thought. *Scott will get the statement, and everything will be fine.*

But everything wasn't fine. There were several horses tied up outside the sheriff's office when they arrived back in town. Once they stepped inside, they found U.S. Marshal David Cotton with two of his deputies.

And with them stood Doogan McConnell.

"That's her," McConnell bellowed, pointing a pudgy finger in Tori's direction. "She's the other pickpocket who made off with my diamond. And there's her thieving brother who escaped from the county jail a few weeks ago!"

Horrified, Tori clung to Billy's side, unable to even defend herself, she was so shocked. His arm came around and rested protectively on her shoulders.

"Marshal, you might want to explain to me why you're here," he said to the lawman, ignoring McConnell's outburst.

"Billy, I'm sorry I had to come down here like this, but McConnell claims Victoria Nelson was the one who stole his diamond tiepin back about two years ago, near Amarillo. We connected her as the third person who'd been with the Nelson brothers during a pickpocketing spree at a town event. They were arrested, but our sources say their brother managed to get away with the diamond." The short, stocky man glanced wryly at Tori. "At least we thought it was a brother."

"Well, this is Kyle Nelson, and he's just turned himself in. They broke out because they say they can prove Tori is innocent of stealing the diamond," Billy supplied.

"I got witnesses that say she has it!" McConnell interjected as he tried to grab Tori by the arm.

Tori recoiled, but the marshal managed to yank the large man back before he reached her. "I don't have it, Marshal. I never did!" she cried out in defense.

The marshal looked at her for a moment and then shifted his gaze to Kyle. "Where is your brother?"

Kyle shook his head. "I can't tell you that, Sir. But I can promise you he'll be back with the truth of what happened. We only broke out to protect our sister."

Tori could feel the tension in the room as the marshal considered what to do. She guessed he was in his midforties because his brown hair was sprinkled with gray and his face was etched with lines around his eyes and on his cheeks. She hoped that wisdom truly did come with age. The marshal sighed as if the weight of the world was on his shoulders, and she had a bad feeling about what he would say next.

"For right now, Billy, you're going to have to lock them both up. The judge will have to work this out when he comes back in town."

She felt Billy tense beside her. "No, Sir, I can't do it," he answered clearly. "I can't arrest her for something I know she didn't do."

Cotton seemed to sympathize with the sheriff, but he wasn't going to soften. "Billy, he's got witnesses that say they saw her with the diamond. You know that she's a thief. You arrested her yourself. It isn't hard to imagine she took the diamond."

She looked up at Billy and noticed his jaw was clenched and his face was set like a stone. "She has been a model citizen for nearly three months now. She knows that if she took the gem, the right thing would be to confess." He looked down at Tori and gave her a reassuring smile. "If she says she didn't take it, I believe her."

"That's a lie! I got witnesses!" McConnell charged again.

"Then your witnesses are the liars here, McConnell!" Billy shot back.

"Now, just hold on here!" Marshal Cotton stepped between them, holding his hands up. "We are going to discuss this like adults." He nodded to McConnell. "Why don't you go and have a seat before you do something that I'm not going to like."

McConnell scowled at the marshal's subtle threat but did as he was told.

Cotton pointed at Billy. "And I want to know why you're so protective of a woman you arrested three months ago yourself. The whole county heard about the ruckus you made about her light sentence, so what's changed?"

"Because now she's my—"

"Marshal!" Tori cried out, stepping away from Billy before he could say any more. She didn't want him to ruin his reputation because of her. If the marshal knew they were engaged, he'd think Billy's judgment was clouded by his feelings for her. "I'm his friend, that's all. He's been helpful in teaching me about the law, and because of that, I've changed my way of thinking. I know it's wrong to steal. And I know it's wrong to lie." She gazed at the marshal imploringly. "I promise you that I didn't take the diamond. I didn't take anything from the town that night. Kyle and Scott had it all. I was purely acting as a decoy."

"Now, Tori, I—" Billy started to say, but once again she stopped him.

"Sheriff Aaron, it's alright. Once Scott arrives with the evidence, this will all be cleared up."

Marshal Cotton looked over at Billy. "Son, I agree it seems unlikely that she has the diamond. . ." McConnell started making protesting noises, but Cotton continued over him, "*but,* where there are witnesses, I've got to respond. If you don't lock her up, I will."

Billy looked more upset than Tori had ever seen him. He grabbed her by the arm and pulled her to him. "There is no way I'm going to allow her to be locked up! You take my badge or whatever you need to do, but she's not—"

"No!" Tori yelled out, pushing herself away from him in a rough motion. "I will not allow you to ruin your career because of me!"

Billy shook his head. "Tori, you're my—"

"I am your friend and nothing more. Now let the marshal do his job," she said plainly, all the while pleading with her eyes for him to understand.

"Listen to the lady, Sheriff. This is a battle you're not going to win," Cotton assured him firmly.

For a moment, she and Billy stared at one another, desperation over the circumstances standing between them like a giant wall, too big to cross or tear down.

Cotton took her gently by the arm and motioned for Kyle to follow him.

"Just pray," she whispered before she turned her head and entered the cell behind her brother.

When the cold, hard clank of the door shutting sounded behind her, she turned to see Marshal Cotton walking over to Billy. "Can I trust that you're going to make sure she stays here until the judge arrives?"

Billy stared at Tori for a long moment before turning his attention back to the marshal. With deliberate motions, he put a hand over the star hanging from his vest and removed it. "No, Sir, you can't," he answered. He removed the pistols, which were the property of the town, and placed them in the marshal's hands alongside the star.

"Son, this is pure foolishness!" Cotton informed him, shaking his head sadly.

But Billy straightened, and with a glint of determination shining in his eyes, he pointed toward the cell. "That woman in there is not just my friend, Marshal, she's my fiancée. And I'm going to do whatever I can to help her brother find proof of her innocence."

"Oh, Billy," Tori cried softly, her eyes blurred with tears.

He held her gaze with love fiercely radiating out to her. "I'll find a way to get you out of there, Sweetheart," he promised before he turned and walked out the door.

Kyle came up and put a comforting arm around her shoulders. "I guess he's not so bad after all."

She wiped at her cheeks and tried to smile. "No. No, he's not bad at all."

He kissed the side of her head and gave her a squeeze. "Don't worry, Sis. We've always had fate on our side."

But Tori shook her head. "Not fate, Kyle. God. We've always had God looking after us, even when I didn't know

Him. And it's God who is going to get us through. We just need to pray."

"I don't know how to pray," Kyle confessed, sounding confused and a little embarrassed.

She hugged him to her side. "That's alright, big brother. I'll teach you."

From the cell next door to them, a raucous voice interrupted them. "I knew you looked familiar. I never forget a face!" Vega crowed, holding onto the bars and pressing his face between them. "You need to be nice to me, little girl, since I'm one of the witnesses who saw you with the diamond."

Kyle walked over to the evil man, poking a finger near his face. "Why don't you go back to whatever hole you crawled out of?"

Vega smiled, his two gold teeth in front gleaming. "Make me, Outlaw."

Tori watched in shock as Kyle's fist shot out and planted itself right into Vega's face, knocking the man to the floor with a resounding thud.

She ran over to the dividing bars and stared down at the unconscious man. "Oh, Kyle. I guess you've never heard of the Golden Rule, have you," she told him, shaking her head.

Kyle rubbed his fist and frowned. "The golden what?"

She smiled at him. "Never mind. That's just one of many things I need to tell you about." She pulled him over to the cot and began to share with him what she'd learned since arriving in Springton.

sixteen

It didn't take long for most of Springton to find out what was going on—or to form their own opinions about whether Tori was guilty or innocent. McConnell stood outside the jail spreading every lie about her he could think up, even claiming she was glad her brothers went to jail so she could have the diamond all to herself.

Tori tried to ignore the gossip, secure in the fact that she would have been the first to turn herself in if it would have helped her brothers.

An hour had passed since her arrest and Billy's departure. From her frequent peeks out the tiny barred window, she knew a crowd was forming outside, some wanting to know why the sheriff left town and others wanting to know more about her arrest.

Just as she began to wonder whether Susannah and Rachel had heard the news yet, they both came barging into the office like soldiers on a mission, pushing aside the deputy who'd been guarding the door.

"We'd like to see Miss Nelson, if you don't mind," Rachel said to Marshal Cotton.

Cotton shook his head. "If I let you see her, the whole town's going to want to come in here. Why don't you come back tomorrow?"

Susannah marched around Rachel and right up to the marshal with her fan in hand. "I don't think you understand,

Marshal. We are her guardians, the very ones who have been looking after her all these months. The judge himself ordered us to stay by her side!"

Cotton, who appeared tired of dealing with the whole fiasco, motioned them toward the jail cells. "Just go, then. But no funny business. No trying to talk me into letting her go or trying to sneak her out."

Appalled, Susannah gasped and put a gloved hand to her throat. "Marshal! Rachel is the reverend's wife, and I am a God-fearing Christian woman!"

Cotton reddened with discomfiture. "Well, pardon me, ladies. Y'all just go on back," he muttered and quickly went over to the other side of the room.

Tori smiled as her two friends made their way over to her. "I thought you'd never get here," Tori told them.

Susannah and Rachel each reached out to grab her hands. "Oh, Sugar, we're so sorry this happened. When Billy told us you'd been arrested and that he'd resigned as sheriff, why I thought surely it must all be a big mistake."

Tori's eyes filled with tears. "Oh, Susannah, I begged him not to, but he wouldn't listen." She shook her head sadly. "This is all my fault."

Rachel squeezed her hand. "Now don't talk like that, Tori. Tommy and Danny told us how Billy feels about you. A man does what he thinks he has to do."

Kyle made a coughing noise behind her, and she realized that she hadn't introduced them to her brother. "Oh! Susannah and Rachel, this is my brother Kyle. Kyle, these are the ladies who have been so kind to me these past months, Susannah Aaron and Rachel Stone."

Kyle shyly approached the women. Nodding his head,

he greeted them. "Nice to meet ya."

Rachel smiled kindly at him. "It's nice to meet you too, Kyle."

"Yes, it is," Susannah added. "I declare, if you two don't look a lot alike!" Her eyes darted back and forth between them. "Does the other brother look like y'all?"

Tori nodded. "All three of us have blond hair. Hopefully, Billy won't have any trouble finding Scott because of that."

Susannah patted her on the cheek. "Now you just never mind about that, Sugar. Billy took all three of his brothers and Reverend Stone with him to track Scott down. If anybody can straighten this mess up, it's the five of them." She winked at Tori. "Especially Billy. I tell you, I've never seen a man so in love—if you don't count my Bobby, that is— with a woman like he is with you. He just needed a little help realizing it, is all."

Tori eyed Susannah suspiciously. "You mean, you had something to do with Billy's sudden proposal of marriage?"

"Goodness, no! I just wanted him to start courting you! He thought up the marriage idea all on his own!"

Tori looked over at Rachel, who just shrugged her shoulders.

It didn't matter who helped Billy, she was just so glad he did love her and wanted to marry her.

If only she could be sure her brother and Billy would come through with getting the proof she needed to be set free. . . .

At midnight, ten miles east of Waco, the men decided to make camp in a small clearing among the tall oak trees lining the dirt road. Tommy made a fire and put on a pot of coffee while the rest of the men unsaddled their horses and tied them up close by to discourage anyone who might want to steal them. Using their saddles as pillows, they laid out their bedrolls by the fire and began to make plans for the following day.

What wasn't surprising was that the preacher was the one to give them the best advice on how to seek someone out who might be hard to find. Not only had he been somewhat of an infamous gunslinger before he was a Christian, he'd also been a bounty hunter. He'd collected quite a fortune, in fact, since he seemed to have a knack for finding his prey.

Billy looked at Reverend Caleb gratefully. "I can't tell you how much I appreciate your help, Pastor. You don't ever talk about your former life, so I know it must be hard to use some of those talents you haven't used in years."

Caleb shook his head. "Think nothing of it, Billy. I am just so thankful that God took me from that kind of life and blessed me with the one I have now. I don't speak of it because my life is so full and blessed now, not because it's painful." He grinned sheepishly. "But you're right. It is a particular talent of mine to seek out outlaws—it's just one that I have little need for anymore."

The brothers laughed at that, but Billy soon sobered. "Maybe you should have made a career as a lawman. It looks like Springton is going to be looking for another sheriff now," he commented morosely.

Bobby gave him a brotherly knock on the shoulder. "Both the preacher and I are on the town council, Billy. I can guarantee that we are not going to accept your hasty, and foolish, I must say, resignation."

Billy bristled at that. "I did what I thought was right."

Tommy shook his head. "You could have done all this *and* stayed on as the sheriff, Billy. Admit it, you just got mad and wanted to make a point."

Billy started to deny it but then realized they were right. Sighing, he admitted, "I guess you're right. I just couldn't believe he was locking Tori up."

Bobby nodded sagely. "We can do some pretty crazy things when we think our women are in trouble. You may recall that shortly after I'd married Susannah, we were held up by stagecoach robbers. Before I could stop her, Susannah had made them mad, so they grabbed her and ran off, shooting me on the side of the head as they rode." He grinned while unconsciously rubbing the old scar at his temple. "I dragged myself up into those woods, bleeding everywhere, and looked for hours, desperate to rescue her before they could hurt her. When I found her, she had already rescued herself and was walking away from their camp. I was actually angry at her for not waiting for me!"

They all laughed, and Danny commented, "You ain't never going to see me acting that crazy over a woman."

Billy snorted. "Famous last words. A man never thinks it can happen to him." He threw a stick in the blazing fire and watched the embers stir and fly away. "I just hope we can find Tori's brother and help him get that statement. I don't know what I'll do if they convict her."

Reverend Caleb patted Billy's shoulder. "Why don't we pray? Worrying never does anything, but prayer can change everything."

They all bowed their heads as the preacher led them in a

prayer seeking guidance and protection—and asking for a small miracle in finding the proof they needed.

☙

After eight days of having to endure the tiny cell and the snide comments from McConnell, who frequented the jail even after bailing out Vega, Tori again prayed that they'd hear from Billy and her brother soon.

Time was running out for them. She'd already plead innocent to the charges, and the jury had been chosen from around the county. Any minute now, her lawyer was going to come into the jail to escort her to the small courthouse down the road.

She could only pray that God would hand her a miracle.

Every day she'd read her Bible and prayed with the ladies, and she could feel God's strength carrying her through, giving her peace and patience. She also rejoiced in the fact that Kyle had accepted Jesus into his heart just the night before.

For days she'd been talking to Kyle, telling him about Jesus and what He meant to her life. Tori couldn't believe it when he asked if she'd help him pray a prayer so he could become a Christian too.

Now, if only she could speak to Scott about her faith!

Standing up from her cot, Tori walked over to the washbasin, which the marshal or his deputy kindly filled with fresh water every morning, and splashed her face.

What she hadn't expected was her story spreading so fast all over East Texas. Rachel and Susannah had brought in articles from Dallas to Houston and towns in between, each story more fantastic than the last. In them she was written up like some sort of fictional character who'd blazed a trail across Texas robbing banks and lifting price-less jewels from the richest folks she could find. They said she'd lived a double life, posing as a boy during her thieving raids and living like a high-society woman the rest of the time.

While Susannah thought it was all sort of funny, Tori was horrified that anyone would think she had actually done all those things instead of being just a petty pick-pocket. The last time she'd made the trek to the court-house, there had been photographers there, urging her to pose for a picture, and reporters yelling questions she wouldn't even deem to answer because they were so ridiculous.

Miss Addie, from the mercantile, had come by to visit, and she was all excited that Tori had become such a celebrity, claiming she caused more commotion than the time Annie Oakley came to town with the Wild West Show years back.

If the jury believed these stories, how would her lawyer ever convince them of her innocence?

"Mr. Washburn! Marshal," she heard Kyle say from behind her as she toweled off her face. "Has there been any word?"

Tori turned to see her lawyer, whom Susannah had hired for her, with Marshal Cotton. Her heart dropped when she saw their grim faces and watched Mr. Washburn shake his head.

"I just came to take Miss Nelson down to the courthouse." Washburn's eyes glanced toward the marshal as if he were reluctant to say any more. "I need to tell you that it's going to be worse than last time. There are reporters here from as far up as Kansas, and even New York has wired saying they were sending reporters down. A writer stopped me on the way in and commented that your life story would make an excellent dime novel adventure." He scratched his gray beard. "It might be a little rough walking into the courtroom."

Tori walked to the bars. "What are the townsfolk saying about Billy?"

Marshal Cotton answered. "Some are clamoring for Cecil Banyan to take over as sheriff." Banyan was a deputy from Tyler who had family and friends here in Springton. "They don't think it was right of Billy to quit just because he thought you were innocent. They think he shouldn't have put his personal feelings above his job," he admitted honestly, although he didn't seem to like it.

It was just as she'd feared. Deep down, she knew they also didn't want him involved with someone of her shady past, especially a woman he himself had arrested.

Kyle jumped to her defense. "Billy had just asked her to marry him! How was he supposed to keep his personal feelings out of it?"

Cotton put up his hands. "I ain't disputing what you're saying. I might have done the same thing, had I been in his situation. I'm just repeating what the talk is."

He took the keys to the cell from his pocket and opened the heavy metal door. Together, Washburn and the marshal escorted Tori to the courthouse, leaving Kyle behind in the jail.

He would be called to testify later, but she wished they'd let him out to be her support. At least Susannah and Rachel were waiting for her outside of the sheriff's office.

They helped shield her from the quizzical crowd and the nosy reporters.

Inside the courtroom, the ladies sat right behind her and kept whispering that everything was going to be all right, encouraging her to believe God would help her through.

Tori knew God was with her. She could feel a peace within her she normally wouldn't be experiencing in such a situation.

Patience, however, was a much-needed commodity as the trial wore on. McConnell had Vega and two other witnesses who said they'd seen her the night her brothers were arrested and that they had seen her with the diamond.

This, of course, was a lie. She knew they had spotted her days later when she'd been talking to her brothers through the jail window late at night. After that, only Vega had truly seen her up close, which is why he recognized her. And they couldn't have seen her with anything remotely resembling a diamond!

When Washburn had his chance to call witnesses, both she and her brother testified, as well as Rachel and Susannah, who were more character witnesses than anything else. But despite their well-worded testimony and positive answers, it didn't seem to be enough.

As the trial wore on, Tori had the awful feeling the jury was not convinced of her innocence in this. Maybe it was the way they looked at her, shaking their heads as if they couldn't imagine how she could steal such a priceless jewel and then let her brothers take the blame for it, not to mention what they'd heard out on the street.

Tori couldn't blame them. From the testimonies of McConnell's men and the circus this trial was creating, she looked so very guilty.

On the third day, when the jury left the room so they could vote on her guilt or innocence, she prepared herself for the worst—a life behind bars. A life without Billy Ray Aaron.

seventeen

"I can't believe we not only tracked down a witness who saw Lachlan take the diamond, but we know the person who bought it from him after he got to Waco!" Tommy marveled as they rode into Springton with their witness in tow.

Reverend Caleb grinned. "It's amazing what a little reward money will do. I learned that among thieves and outlaws, you're loyal to the highest bidder." He shook his head at Billy and glanced back to their quiet witness. "I still think you could've gotten away with five hundred dollars instead of a full thousand!"

Billy tipped his hat upward a little to wipe the sweat from his forehead. "I'd have paid more to get the right information."

Scott Nelson, who rode with them, studied Billy from his borrowed horse. "I still don't understand why Tori would get herself engaged to a sheriff. She normally avoids you lawmen like the plague. Are you sure you're shooting straight with me?" he asked suspiciously.

Danny laughed. "You had to be there to believe it. I've never seen two people fight falling in love like they did."

Billy's brothers and the preacher all laughed at that.

"Alright, alright. So I'm a little slow on the uptake. But you don't have to worry, Scott, about me being a sheriff. I doubt the town will want me back after this."

Scott looked a lot like Tori with his striking blond hair,

but his eyes were light green instead of blue. He was tall and more muscular than Kyle was. He seemed more serious too. "I don't care what you are, just as long as you take care of my sister. She didn't have much of a choice when we taught her how to steal. Me and Kyle were wrong to do it, but it was the only way we knew how to survive."

"She told us all about it, Scott. We're just glad she got caught in Springton and not some other town that might not have been so lenient," Reverend Caleb commented.

They were just riding onto the main street when they spotted the crowd outside the jail.

"What in the world. . . ?" Bobby commented with disbelief.

Billy looked at the men with him in alarm. "They've already started the trial!" He snapped at his reins and dug his heels into the side of his horse, Jericho. "Let's go," he yelled as he galloped at breakneck speed toward the courthouse.

The crowd's interest immediately turned from the windows they'd been peering into toward the riders bearing down on them. Jumping from their horses, the Springton men, along with Scott and their witness, were unprepared for the barrage of questions they were suddenly pounded with.

"Are you Billy Aaron? The sheriff who gave up his job because of the lady outlaw, Tori Nelson?" asked a short, black-haired man as he stepped in front of Billy.

Billy, taken aback, could only sputter, "What?"

"Tell us, Sir! Just how much money does she have hidden from all her bank heists?" another called out.

"Who told you she robbed a—" he started to ask.

"Is it true she and her brothers once ran with the Dalton gang?"

"The Dal. . ." He choked with disbelief. Shaking his head with irritation, Billy shoved the reporters out of his way with the help of his brothers. "Get out of the way," he growled, pushing the courthouse door open.

Once Billy was inside, the judge immediately started banging his gavel to quiet the excitement his appearance had created in the room. "Billy Ray Aaron, do you and your friends have a reason for disrupting my courtroom?" Judge Denton barked while peering over his spectacles.

Billy wasted no time in walking toward the bench, catching a quick look at Tori's hopeful expression as he passed her. "Your Honor, I've got a witness whose testimony will prove that Tori Nelson did not steal Doogan McConnell's diamond tiepin," he proclaimed ardently. His whole being was focused on getting this whole ordeal resolved.

But Judge Denton shook his head. "Son, you've given me more grief over this woman. First, you want me to throw her in jail; now, you resign your job and go gallivanting all over here and yonder to keep her from going to jail." Billy didn't say anything but just stared intently at the judge for a long moment. Finally the judge sighed. "Alright. Let's hear what this witness has to say."

Diego Rodriquez proceeded to tell of Lachlan McConnell hiring him to lift the diamond tiepin off Doogan McConnell when he wasn't looking. Then Lachlan and his men left Amarillo and headed down to Waco, where he sold the diamond and bought a saloon and hotel.

It was then that Billy presented the judge with the

sworn statement of the man who bought the diamond from Lachlan.

Reverend Caleb stepped up and further explained. "Your Honor, we alerted the authorities in Waco of the theft, and they now have Lachlan McConnell in custody." He looked to Scott, who stood by him. "I'd like to comment also on the bravery of Scott and Kyle Nelson, who broke out of prison only to protect their sister, knowing full well what the consequences of their actions would be. When they heard she was in danger, they immediately set out to find the real thief. As the pastor of Springton and a member of the town council, I'd like to recommend that their breakout not be counted against them and that their sentences be reduced to time served, considering that they both turned themselves in after helping to bring the real thief to justice, which is what they intended to do all along."

The judge nodded. "Duly noted." He let out a deep breath as he gave Tori a long, studying look. "Well, Miss Nelson, in light of this new testimony, I'm going to dismiss the charges against you."

Susannah and Rachel both squealed with delight as they shot up out of their seats to hug her.

The judge pounded heavily on his bench. "However! I want your solemn oath you will never do anything to warrant standing up in this courtroom again! Frankly, I've had enough of both you and Mr. Aaron to last me awhile," he said with heavy irony. "Now, even though you are found innocent in this room, out there you're going to have to live down what those newspapers have built you up to be. Folks may never believe you didn't steal a fortune in jewels or rob banks." He peered meaningfully at Billy. "I hope you'll be able to deal with this, Son, *without* dragging me into it!"

Banging his gavel down once more, he bellowed, "Court's adjourned!"

Those words, acting as dynamite under Billy's feet, propelled him to run to Tori and grab her up in his arms.

Hearing her surprised laughter in his ear and the sweet feeling of her arms wrapped around his neck made him realize how much he'd missed her. Those eleven days had been the longest of his life, and he vowed many times that he'd never leave her again.

He finally put her down, after a none-too-gentle elbow in the ribs from Susannah, and took her hands into his own.

"Are you alright? They didn't mistreat you while I was gone, did they?" he asked, searching her face with concern.

She shook her head, smiling at him with love dancing in her eyes. "I'm fine, Billy. I had my brother in there with me, and Susannah and Rachel kept us company all the time." She squeezed his hands gently. "What about you? I was so scared you'd be hurt."

"Hunting down information and dealing with criminals is nothing new to me, Tori. As a deputy, I was involved in situations far more dangerous than this."

"Are you going to hog her all to yourself, Lawman? It's only been a few days for you, but it's two years since I've seen her," Scott's dry voice spoke from beside them.

"Scott!" Tori cried as she threw herself into her brother's waiting arms. Billy watched with a fond smile as she greeted Scott and spoke with him a few minutes before Marshal Cotton had to take him back to the jail.

When the crowd began to thin out, Billy grabbed Tori's

hand again. "Let's go out the back. They'll never leave us alone if we go out there," he told her wryly, nodding toward the entrance of the courtroom. "You're quite the celebrity, you know."

As they weaved their way toward the door, he heard Tori groan. "Can you believe what they're saying about me? Next, they'll be accusing me of rustling cattle, for goodness' sake!"

Billy peeked out the door, and when he saw the coast was clear, he pulled her along with him, heading toward the hill to his nearly completed house. "Aw, don't worry, Darlin'. By next month, they'll all have forgotten it and moved on to the next big story."

She made a "humph" sound. "Not quite, seeing as there's a fellow wanting to write a dime novel about my so-called infamous exploits!"

Billy laughed and let go of her hand, putting his arm around her instead. "Well, it can be something we can show to our children."

She stopped him and turned so they were facing one another. "Speaking of my reputation, what are we going to do if the town council and the rest of the town make a fuss about you being reinstated as sheriff?"

He reached up and framed her face, rubbing his thumbs softly across her smooth, sun-kissed cheeks. "Tori, Darlin', we are going to take things as they come and just trust God that He's going to make a way for both of us."

She turned her head and kissed his palm. "You're right. We're not trusting God to do His work if we worry. Susannah and Rachel have told me that often enough."

Staring deep into her eyes, Billy couldn't help but feel

profoundly blessed to have her in his life. The love he felt for her seemed to fill every part of his being to near bursting.

To his surprise, Tori stood up on her toes and kissed him. Closing his eyes, he responded to the sweet, shy movement of her lips, reveling in the fact that she was his—soon she'd be his wife. He then showered soft kisses on her cheeks, eyes, and nose before returning to her mouth once again.

After that, he stood quietly for a moment, holding her in his arms, so grateful that with God's help they'd been able to keep her out of jail. Now, their dream of a life together could become reality.

"I love you, Tori, with all my heart," he whispered in her ear, feeling the overpowering need to convey what he was feeling. But even those heartfelt words seemed inadequate.

"And I love you, Billy, more than I thought was possible," she responded, her tone unstable, as if she, too, were having the same problem.

Billy gave her one more kiss before he reluctantly stepped back. "Come see where we'll live. If the carpenters have done as I asked, you'll be happily surprised."

Together they walked up the hill to the ranch-style house. Just as he'd asked for, large windows had been cut all around the house, and shiny new panes reflected the afternoon sun. "I know how you hate being indoors, so I thought I'd put windows all around, hoping they would help keep you from feeling too closed in," he explained as they walked inside.

They walked along the polished wood floor to the back of the house. "We'll go into Dallas for furniture, and I want you to choose whatever you like. The kitchen cabinets aren't finished yet, either, but they should be ready in time for our wedding."

She glanced up at him with raised eyebrows. "And when is our wedding?"

He winked at her. "As soon as we can arrange it, Darlin'. Now that you're a free woman, I don't want to take the chance of some other fellow coming along and asking to court you!"

She smiled at him cheekily. "You don't have to worry about that as long as you behave yourself and act nice!"

"Just stay away from making fun of our sacred Texas laws, then."

She laughed, but as soon as they stepped into the room at the back of the house, her laughter drifted into a gasp. The ceiling of the octagon-shaped room was well over fifteen feet high, and huge windows that nearly reached from the ceiling to the floor surrounded them, giving them a panoramic view of the woods, as well as the town below.

"We'll have curtains to close off the windows for privacy, of course, but anytime you feel closed in or get a hankering for the outdoors, just open them up."

She looked around at the room with awe in her eyes and then gazed up at him. "Thank you, Billy. But I don't understand how you ordered all this. You didn't have time before you left town."

He grinned at her, feeling a little embarrassed. "I told them to build it this way long before I would admit to myself I was falling in love with you," he admitted. "Somewhere in the back of my mind I must have known you would be sharing this house with me."

He stepped behind her and wrapped his arms around her waist, resting her shoulders against his chest as they stood gazing out the windows. "I thank God you arrested me on that day three months ago, Billy. If you hadn't, I would have never become a Christian and probably would still be running around dressed like a boy and stinking like a skunk." They laughed, and she continued, "And I wouldn't have become engaged to the most wonderful man in the world."

"You weren't thinking I was wonderful three months ago."

"No," she admitted with a giggle. "But it's true what Reverend Caleb often says. God has a reason for everything that happens. Sometimes it's hard to see it, at first. But if we're patient and stay thankful to Him, we will."

"How did you get so wise?" He kissed her hair.

"I had a good teacher."

"Thanks, Darlin'," he answered smugly.

She reached up and tweaked his arm with a soft pinch. "I was talking about the preacher, Reverend Caleb! I'm afraid your law lessons didn't leave me anything but bored." She twisted her head to give him a quick peck on the chin. "But it was worth enduring to spend time with you."

He laughed at her bluntness. "Don't worry. I know enough about the law to keep you out of trouble."

She grasped his hands, which were folded around her. "I sure hope and pray you'll get the chance to be the sheriff again so you can practice your law."

He wanted that too, with all his heart. But if he never got to wear the silver star again, he would be happy. He had his family, Tori's love, and the promises of God. He couldn't ask for more than that.

epilogue

Three months later, the dime novel *The Outrageous Adventures of Texas Tori* hit the stands and was an instant success. The quiet town of Springton became a favorite stopover on the train route for the novel's fans. Each one hoped to catch a glimpse of the famous lady outlaw who married a sheriff and her two outlaw brothers who were now being trained as deputies!

Addie Norton was quick to capitalize on the flood of tourism by setting up a newsstand that carried the paperback, plus copies of all the articles that had been printed about Tori during and after the trial.

Tori didn't know what to do about the exaggeration of her criminal past and all the excitement it was causing. She was glad the town's businesses were profiting and growing, but she hated having to sneak around just to go see her husband at the sheriff's office or simply go to the mercantile for supplies!

Standing at one of the large picture windows, she sipped on a cup of coffee, watching the crowded streets of the town below. She heard a sound from behind her and wasn't surprised when Billy reached around and circled her waist with one arm, while tucking a daisy behind her ear with the other.

"Good morning, darlin' wife," he drawled as he nuzzled her cheek against his freshly shaven face.

She leaned back into her husband of one month and sighed happily. "You wouldn't happen to know who brought in a stack of those worthless dime novels and put them on the kitchen table, would you?" she asked him calmly.

She felt the rumble of his chuckle. "Those are to pass out to our children and grandchildren when we are old and gray so they can know what kind of woman their ma and grandma was in her younger days."

He grunted when she nudged him in the side with her elbow. "The only truths in that novel are where it states you married me and the town still wanted you for their sheriff. And, of course, where Scott and Kyle were released from prison and you hired them on as deputies."

"I figure if they know how a thief thinks, they'll be better at catching them. With the influx of people we've had lately, I can almost guarantee they'll come in handy," he reasoned.

"You're trying to get me off the subject, Lawman. I want you to take that untruthful stack of lies and burn them! I want our children and grandchildren to think I'm a lady, not an outlaw!"

He kissed her cheek. "You are a lady in the truest sense of the word, Darlin'. No dime novel is going to take that away. And besides," he teased, "since you've mended your ways and are walking the straight and narrow, they'll go away when you don't give them anything else to write about."

Turning in his embrace, Tori placed her coffee cup on a nearby table, then wrapped her arms around his neck. "I just thank God we have each other and that He worked everything out."

Hugging her close, Billy told her, "I thank Him every day, Darlin'—every single day."

KANSAS

*S*urviving the harsh prairie elements—like surviving the storms of the heart—takes faith and determination, which four young women need to prove they possess. Can their hearts hold fast against the gales that buffet them? Will they find love waiting at the end of the storm?

Love on the Kansas prairie is hard and unpredictable. . .but also as inevitable as an early summer cyclone. Watch in wonder as God turns the storms of life into seasons of growth and joy.

paperback, 464 pages, 5 ³⁄₁₆" x 8"

$\mathcal{A}$ $\mathcal{L}$etter $\mathcal{T}$o $\mathcal{O}$ur $\mathcal{R}$eaders

Dear Reader:

In order that we might better contribute to your reading enjoyment, we would appreciate your taking a few minutes to respond to the following questions. We welcome your comments and read each form and letter we receive. When completed, please return to the following:

Rebecca Germany, Fiction Editor
Heartsong Presents
PO Box 719
Uhrichsville, Ohio 44683

1.   Did you enjoy reading *The Sheriff and the Outlaw* by Kimberley Comeaux?

   ❏ Very much! I would like to see more books by this author!
   ❏ Moderately. I would have enjoyed it more if

_____

_____

2.   Are you a member of **Heartsong Presents**?   Yes ❏ No ❏
   If no, where did you purchase this book?_____

_____

3.   How would you rate, on a scale from 1 (poor) to 5 (superior), the cover design?_____

4.   On a scale from 1 (poor) to 10 (superior), please rate the following elements.

   _____ Heroine   _____ Plot

   _____ Hero   _____ Inspirational theme

   _____ Setting   _____ Secondary characters

5. These characters were special because_____
   _____
   _____

6. How has this book inspired your life?_____
   _____
   _____

7. What settings would you like to see covered in future
   Heartsong Presents books?_____
   _____
   _____

8. What are some inspirational themes you would like to see
   treated in future books?_____
   _____
   _____

9. Would you be interested in reading other **Heartsong
   Presents** titles?   Yes ❏   No ❏

10. Please check your age range:
    ❏ Under 18   ❏ 18-24   ❏ 25-34
    ❏ 35-45   ❏ 46-55   ❏ Over 55

Name _____

Occupation _____

Address _____

City _____ State _____ Zip _____

Email _____

Presents

Great Inspirational Romance at a Great Price!

Heartsong Presents books are inspirational romances in contemporary and historical settings, designed to give you an enjoyable, spirit-lifting reading experience. You can choose wonderfully written titles from some of today's best authors like Peggy Darty, Sally Laity, Tracie Peterson, Colleen L. Reece, Lauraine Snelling, and many others.

When ordering quantities less than twelve, above titles are $2.95 each.
Not all titles may be available at time of order.

Hearts♥ng Presents
Love Stories Are Rated G!

That's for godly, gratifying, and of course, great! If you love a thrilling love story but don't appreciate the sordidness of some popular paperback romances, **Heartsong Presents** is for you. In fact, **Heartsong Presents** is the *only inspirational romance book club* featuring love stories where Christian faith is the primary ingredient in a marriage relationship.

Sign up today to receive your first set of four never-before-published Christian romances. Send no money now; you will receive a bill with the first shipment. You may cancel at any time without obligation, and if you aren't completely satisfied with any selection, you may return the books for an immediate refund!

Imagine. . .four new romances every four weeks—two historical, two contemporary—with men and women like you who long to meet the one God has chosen as the love of their lives. . .all for the low price of $9.97 postpaid.

To join, simply complete the coupon below and mail to the address provided. **Heartsong Presents** romances are rated G for another reason: They'll arrive *Godspeed!*

YES! Sign me up for Heartsong!

NEW MEMBERSHIPS WILL BE SHIPPED IMMEDIATELY!
Send no money now. We'll bill you only $9.97 post-paid with your first shipment of four books. Or for faster action, call toll free 1-800-847-8270.

NAME _____

ADDRESS _____

CITY _____ STATE _____ ZIP _____

MAIL TO: HEARTSONG PRESENTS, PO Box 721, Uhrichsville, Ohio 44683

YES10-96